# THANK YOU,
# GOOD-BYE

OTHER BOOKS
IN THE SERIES

# THANK YOU, GOOD-BYE

# GOOD-BYE

## J. B. JENKINS

Thomas Nelson Publishers
*Nashville*

Published in Nashville, Tennessee, by Thomas Nelson,
Inc., and distributed in Canada by Lawson Falle, Ltd.,
Cambridge, Ontario.

### Library of Congress
### Cataloging-in-Publication Data

Jenkins, Jerry B.
    [Shannon]
    Thank you, good-bye / by J. B. Jenkins.
       p.   cm. — (Margo mysteries : 7)
    Originally published: Shannon. Chicago : Moody
Press, 1979.
    ISBN 0-8407-3234-1 (pbk.)
    1. Detective and mystery stories, American.
I. Title.  II. Series: Jenkins, Jerry B.
Margo mysteries : vol. 7.
PS3560.E485S5   1991
813'.54—dc20                                        91–18584
                                                              CIP

Printed in the United States of America

1 2 3 4 5 6 7 — 96 95 94 93 92 91

# ONE

I had driven Margo to her apartment and had even ridden the elevator to her floor. I walked her to her door, and we joked about whether I should also check every room in her apartment before feeling confident about leaving her.

"And even if I do," I said, "who'll see *me* home?"

We were more than thirty miles from the scene of the last unsolved slaying in a series of six, yet the fear we covered with nervous humor reached from the heart of Chicago to every suburb.

Though the murders had been linked because of bizarre clues, there was little other pattern. All had occurred within ten miles of the Loop, the last two right downtown.

Four of the six victims had been men. A four-month gap separated the first and second murders; two days separated the second and third. The last three were three to four weeks apart. The most recent just two nights before.

Not that it was easy to know if the murders were actually taking place at night. Nighttime seems to fit our fears of mass murderers, but in reality the times of death were difficult to pinpoint. All anyone knew—and because of the media coverage, everyone knew—was that six people of different ages, backgrounds, occupations, and economic means had been shot through the back of the head apparently by someone they trusted enough to allow into their homes or apartments.

There had been no evidence of struggle, and while the perpetrator had not seemed to move the bodies an inch from where they had fallen, he or she had tidied up each scene with the victim's own dish towels and water. The spent slug of a .357 magnum high-velocity shell, which in one case had been fired from such close range it destroyed the victim's brain before passing through both sides of a wall and imbedding itself in a door jamb, was always removed from the scene. Authorities knew the size of the slug because of careful studies of trajectory and damage to both the victim and the room. And because of one other puzzling fact.

Although the murderer took great pains to dig the slug out of the wall or the door, and in one case even the ceiling, he or she also was careful to leave one empty shell in the victim's hand. Etched onto each shell, apparently with a vibrating tool used to identify appliances, was a squiggly but unmistakable, carefully marked message in tiny block letters: "THANK YOU, S.D."

Even on the placid streets of the affluent North Shore there had been the usual run on dead bolt locks and peepholes. Few people went out alone after dark.

Margo and I had discussed the case for hours fearing that, despite our titles as private investigators for the EH Detective Agency, we had little more insight into these bizarre events than anyone else reading the papers every day.

She leaned back against the wall in the hall outside her

door, and I stood with my face close to hers. "So, when are we gonna get married again?" I said, changing the subject.

"Oh, ho! Again?"

"You know what I mean. When are we going to get engaged again?"

"When you're ready."

"I'm ready," I said.

"And when you ask."

"I'm asking."

"You're not ready."

I rolled my eyes. I could have been irritated with her, but I wasn't. I deserved it. The last time we'd been engaged she had asked for some time to think things over and get her mind settled. Hurt, I had immediately begun seeing someone else.

By the time I realized what I had done to us and quit trying to blame it on her, she had learned a thing or two about dealing with me. We'd been seeing each other again for several months, and there was little doubt in anyone's mind that we would be married, but she was not pushing anything. I was, but I wasn't seriously worried about the outcome.

She smiled up at me. "Good things come to those—"

"Oh, now you've classified yourself as a good thing," I said.

"You got it, pal." She is so beautiful when she's mischievous, so much sweeter than in the past when her tone was edged with sarcasm.

I asked if she wanted me to check out her apartment. "No," she said. "I carry more weapons than you do."

She was right. We both carried handguns, of course, but she also had a whistle and a pretty little decorator tear gas dispenser. "Someday you're gonna mistake that for cologne and set yourself free with it," I said.

"Are you still planning to see Earl at the office tonight?" she asked.

I looked at my watch. "Yeah. Gotta go. You sure you'll be all right?"

"Of course," she said, cupping my face in her hands. "I love you, Philip Spence."

Earl Haymeyer and I live in the same two-story building that houses his detective agency. His apartment is just down the hall from mine, but we're not exactly just another pair of tenants. He owns the building, and all the shop owners on the first floor pay their rent to him.

Not yet forty, Earl has a wealth of law enforcement experience that makes him a great guy to work for and learn from. He can make me feel younger than the ten years that separate us, but he's never condescending. He's all cop, and he's brilliant.

I was surprised to find him with Larry Shipman, who—besides our matronly receptionist, Bonnie—is Earl's only other employee, an investigator like Margo and me. "I thought you had to be up early tomorrow morning, Lar," I said, pushing open the double glass doors to our outer office and shedding my trench coat.

Neither responded. "I'm sorry," I said. "Am I interrupting?"

"Nah," Larry said. "Change of plans. I'm not going back down to my apartment tonight anyway. I'm staying with Earl."

"Afraid of the 'Thank-You Shooter,' huh?" I teased, drawing only a cold look from Earl. Shipman hadn't even looked at me since I walked in the door. "Whoa, I'm sorry, guys," I said, quickly slipping my coat back on. "Gimme a call if you need me."

"Oh, sit down, Spence," Shipman said. "You're gonna hafta know about all this eventually anyway."

Earl stood and motioned us to follow him past the four desks in the outer office and past the darkroom into his private office. Shipman, as usual, wore his off-duty jeans, flannel shirt, armless insulated vest, and construction boots. The most casual I had ever seen Earl was when he took off the jacket of his three-piece suit and rolled up his shirt sleeves. Tonight the jacket was off but the sleeves were down.

It was unlike either of these two to keep secrets. The agency had always worked as a team, almost a family. Though Larry lived in Chicago and the rest of us lived in or around Glencoe, we were tight.

Earl had reminded us time and again that we were not working on the mass murder case, but newspaper photos of the victims and details of each crime were tacked on his wall. Just two days before, during our staff meeting, he had added the latest victim, listed personal characteristics, and allowed us to brainstorm for a while, "just for practice."

We couldn't be officially involved in the investigation because it was Chicago Police Department business and was, of course, being handled by the Homicide Division. Anyway, we had our own caseload to worry about, and although none of our current projects was anywhere near as provocative as the one on everybody's lips, we were busy enough.

I think Earl knew we'd be trying out our own hypotheses on each other all day long if he didn't give us a chance to gas about it as a group once in a while.

"Your news or mine?" Shipman asked Earl as I tried to appear patient.

"Mine," Earl said. "Philip, you know how much heat has been on the Chicago P.D. since the second murder?"

"Yeah, even since the first."

"OK, but it's been building, and the department is really feeling it. It's not just the public, but also the media, the mayor's office, everybody. And with good reason. I mean, it's not that Homicide isn't doing the job, but this is a tough one, and if they don't get some results soon, heads are going to roll."

"Is your old friend Festschrift getting any heat?"

"They all are. He's not heading up the investigation, you know, but he's in the middle of it."

Sergeant Walvoord F. Festschrift had been Earl's commanding officer when Earl was a young cop, several years before Earl left the department to join the state attorney's office as an investigator. In fact, when I met Earl he was special investigator for the U.S. Attorney for Northern Illinois, James A. Hanlon. When Hanlon announced what turned out to be a successful run for governor, Haymeyer went into private practice and opened our agency.

"I spoke with Wally Festschrift a few days ago, Philip," Earl continued. "I offered to help, but we both knew that was impossible. The Homicide boys are embarrassed enough that they don't have any solid leads without having to admit they're seeking the advice of private detectives."

"So he doesn't want your help?"

"It's not that. He'd love all the help he can get, but there probably isn't another man down there who'd stand still for it. The problem is, and Wally doesn't even know this yet, Jim Hanlon called me today and he wants us involved."

I shook my head. "The governor can involve us in a city police matter?"

"The governor can do just about what he pleases in this state, within reason. He offered state assistance early on in the investigation, but the mayor coldly accused him of political maneuvering and said that when the city needed help, it would ask for it. The fact that the murders have all taken place within the city would make it difficult for Hanlon to push state detectives into the picture. He tried to assure the mayor he wasn't trying to embarrass anyone, and to hear him tell it, all he really cares about is the safety of the public."

"You know him, Earl," I said. "Is he genuine?"

"Oh, yeah, I have no doubt about that. That's why he's asking us to become involved. The state will pay for it, but anything we get has to be carefully fed to Chicago, and no one can know."

"It sounds impossible," I said. "What can we do that Chicago can't do? And how can we do anything without their permission? We need information. We need access. You can't get that without arousing suspicion.

"Not without Festschrift we can't," Earl said.

"But you just said he agreed that our involvement would be impossible."

"Only if the brass know we're involved. I'm going to ask him if he'll consider me a consultant. He's at a level where he doesn't have to clear the use of every expert or contact he might employ. He won't pay us. We'll be invisible, for the most part." Haymeyer and Shipman traded glances. "No one will be embarrassed, yet we'll have the access we need."

"Even to the murder scenes?"

"Probably."

"And what happens to Festschrift if anyone finds out he's cooperating with the state? I can just see the headlines."

"Festschrift can't know. That's one of Hanlon's conditions."

"You're not going to tell your old friend that you're using him to make money off the state?"

"I'm hardly doing it to make money, Philip. You know better than that. Hanlon couldn't pay me enough for the cases we'll have to postpone, let alone the ones we'll have to reject."

"You're going to put everybody on this?"

"Of course."

"I can't believe Festschrift won't get suspicious of all the time and effort he sees on our part," I said.

"I know," Earl said. "He's good enough to sniff anything out, but it's as important to us as it is to everyone else involved that no one know the basis of our interest. He must see little effort on our part and must view me as just an interested observer."

"Earl," I said, "you know I think you can do anything, but I just don't see how you're going to be able to pull this off. Hardly a cop in Chicago even takes his day off anymore. They've got everybody on the case. The biggest job they've got is just coordinating all the activity. How can we help without being in the way, and what in the world can we do without anyone knowing?"

"That's where you come in," Shipman said without emotion and still without looking at me.

I stared at him, then back at Earl.

"That's right," Earl said. "Festschrift likes you, right?"

"Well, yeah, but . . ."

"He likes you, right?"

"Well, we only worked on the one case together, and—"

"And he has you just a little underrated, doesn't he?" Earl pressed.

This was something I could warm up to. Festschrift *had*

always called me Kid and seemed surprised whenever I came up with anything of value.

"Yeah," I said tentatively, more as permission to continue than in agreement.

"I'm asking Wally to take you under his wing for a few months in a special internship program I'm initiating for my junior guy."

"C'mon, Earl. I've lived with that junior business for so long it's getting old. I know Larry's been around longer and all that, but haven't I earned a spot yet?"

Shipman broke in, finally looking at me. "Philip, listen. This has nothing to do with the way we feel about you. Your place here is secure. We're thrilled with your progress."

I looked pained.

"OK," Larry said, "not just your progress. We feel you've arrived." He looked to Earl for confirmation, and Earl nodded. Larry continued. "Earl's idea is to play on Festschrift's view of you. He'll buy the internship thing, let you spend time with him and all that, and won't suspect anything. In fact, he'll *want* you to share things with Earl and will likely pump you for Earl's reactions. Sort of a non-threatening way to get help."

"Sure, OK, but will you have to deceive him, lie to him to get him to agree to this?"

"Me?" Earl said, feigning wounded feelings. Even Larry almost grinned. "No, in fact, not even *your* lily-white principles will be violated. I really am initiating such a program. It'll be good for you; it'll go on your record and into your résumé if you're smart. It'll make you a better investigator. You'll have to give me oral and written reports on what you learn."

I was catching on. "And in the process, you'll get

enough information so everyone on our team will be able to get their heads together on the Thank-You Shooter case."

"You got it, pal," I heard for the second time that night.

I sat back, thinking. "So you're going to suggest to Wally that I tag along with him for the next couple of months, or until the case breaks." Earl nodded. I continued. "Meanwhile, I'll be coming back to you with every tidbit we turn up, and you'll be trying to feed back to Wally, through me, anything that might help him—and thus Homicide Division, Chicago P.D., and the mayor—solve the case by himself but really with the help of the governor, who doesn't want any credit."

"It does sound preposterous, I guess," Earl said. "But that's basically it."

"Do I have a choice?" I asked.

"Not really. You don't want to do it?"

"It's not that. It just has to sink in."

"Fair enough. We can settle on the details tomorrow. I want to meet with everyone here to go over the case one more time anyway. Margo knows nothing about this yet."

I nodded. "Now," I said, "Larry has news too, right? Something that's got him so troubled it's affected his sense of humor and even his ability to look me in the face. I hope it's not a problem with me."

"Of course not," Larry said, irritated. "It's just the kind of news I wish I didn't have. Even before you start running around with Festschrift, provided Earl can talk him into that, we already have some information you can feed him."

"You've already got something on the murder case for Festschrift?"

"Do I ever."

# TWO

I had met Larry Shipman long before the EH Detective
Agency had been formed. I was a freelance artist in At-
lanta and was awkwardly trying to help my new friend
Margo Franklin unravel some of the most complicated personal problems I had ever encountered.

Her mother was a circuit court judge in Chicago and
was mixed up with the mob and even a murder. Anyway,
Earl Haymeyer, then of the U.S. Attorney's office, was assigned to the case. In the process of the investigation he
used a freelance media junkie, journalist, informant: Larry
Shipman.

What a character Shipman was. He liked to be near the
action, regardless of what the action was. He was convinced that more happened with the police and the news
media than anywhere. So he taught himself to write, became a stringer for one of the big Chicago dailies, and
hung around radio and television stations long enough to
pick up the technical know-how to handle writing and re-
porting for them too.

But his area of expertise for Earl's purpose back then
was as an informant. With his ability to look any part, he

posed as a convict and Earl got him put in the same cell as a hit man for the mob. Later he helped expose embezzlers at a downtown bank by working for several weeks as a teller. Larry helped me with the first case I ever had as a private detective. I'll never forget climbing down from a second-floor apartment patio into his waiting arms and both of us tumbling down an embankment, laughing our heads off while trying to remain undetected.

Larry wasn't the moody type. He was usually up. He wasn't a Christian by any means, yet he wasn't hostile either. He carefully stayed out of the discussions about God that Margo and I frequently had with Earl. We figured when he wanted to talk about it, he would. He was basically an honest guy and had a real sense of justice, a prerequisite for working for Earl. He didn't have any obvious vices or bad habits, though we knew he dated several different women and never seemed to develop a relationship.

He seemed to genuinely like everyone he worked with. He was particularly good to Bonnie, our receptionist, a widow who has had a rough life. Basically, we all like Ship, and because he's so steady, his mood shifts are very noticeable. Right now, I was noticing.

"I have a friend," Larry began, "well, not a friend actually. More just an acquaintance. Her name is Shannon Perry and she's a newswriter for WMTR-FM, Metro Radio in the city. I never dated her or anything, but I worked on a few stories with her a couple of years ago when I was stringing for Metro. She's a good kid. Kinda straight. Real ambitious. Cute."

Larry stood and went around Earl's desk, stopping directly behind Earl, which Earl doesn't like, but he didn't complain this time. Larry studied each face of the victims pinned to the corkboard. I wanted to ask if he thought this girl knew anything or was involved or what, but Earl is usually the one who pushes Larry to get to the point. I figured if he could be patient, I could too.

"The only one I have ever seen before was number five here," Larry said quietly. It wasn't like him to let his work get to him. I didn't know why he mentioned it again. We all knew he had had a nodding acquaintance with Frances Downs, the twenty-six-year-old producer of local TV shows for Channel 8. Frances was one of the murder victims.

"Did your friend, uh, Shannon, know Frances Downs too?" I tried, but Earl shushed me with a look and a gesture.

"Yeah, uh-huh," Larry said finally. "They knew each other slightly, about as well as Shannon and I knew each other."

I was in an interrogating mood, but Earl was still staring me down, so I waited.

"Shannon swore me to secrecy, Earl," Larry said, suddenly louder and turning to face the boss.

Earl leaned back in his chair and blankly returned the stare. "You said yourself you would break a confidence only for a good reason. I think this is good enough. You told me, it was your idea to tell Philip, and tomorrow you're going to tell Margo."

Larry sat on a corner of Earl's desk, another pet peeve Earl now chose to ignore. Shipman's shoulders sagged. "Shannon lives on the far north side, almost into Evanston," he said.

He said that simply, as if it had significance in itself. I had to think about it for a minute. The first Thank-You murder had taken place up there somewhere. "How far from where this Ng guy was killed?" I asked.

Larry looked at me squarely and recited the facts the

way Earl often did. "Lawson Ng, Filipino male, age thirty-three, slight build, athletic, bachelor, Park District recreational director six years, found murdered in his second-floor apartment Wednesday, June 2, by a bullet wound through the brain from the back of his head, a wound the coroner says was inflicted most likely during the day on Tuesday, the first."

I knew all that. "So," I said, "how far from—"

"Same block," Larry said coldly.

"Wow."

"Yeah, wow. Some coincidence, huh?"

"Could be," I said. "Surely it's not unusual to have a crime committed in one's neighborhood, and it's not really that bizarre to have slightly known someone who became a victim. Are you trying to make something of the fact that this Shannon has had some kind of connection with two of the victims?"

Larry and Earl glanced at each other. "I wouldn't," Larry admitted, "if that was all there is to it. The thing is, Shannon herself is obsessed by it. I've never seen her this way. I mean, like I say, I don't know her that well, but she's usually just a nut, a fun-loving type who's a good little writer and has a real future."

"Well, *you're* apparently convinced there's nothing to the coincidence, so can't you just talk her out of worrying about it? Or *are* you worried about it?"

"Let him finish, Philip," Earl said. "There's much more to this, or Larry wouldn't be giving it a second thought."

Larry seemed detached again, standing and looking again at the board. He faced the wall as he spoke. "Victim number two, Annamarie Matacena, Italian female, age fifty-one, heavy build, divorced, nurses' aide in the pediatric ward, Mid-City Hospital on the near north side, found murdered in her tiny uptown apartment, same method of operation, apparently on her day off, Thursday, September 2."

We'd been over these facts so many times; I wanted to say something, but Earl was indulging Larry still. I let him talk.

"Shannon knew this woman, too," he said. "She had almost forgotten about it and probably wouldn't have put it together except that the picture in the paper brought it back to her."

"Where did she know her from?" I asked.

"Shannon was researching an in-depth piece on Mid-City's care of handicapped children, and while Mrs. Matacena was not interviewed, she was assigned to help Shannon find her way around for an hour or so."

It was a wild coincidence, but I was still having trouble worrying too much about it. What was Larry saying? What was Shannon saying? Did she feel she ought to be under suspicion? Was she worried that some strange second nature overtook her and that she herself was murdering these acquaintances?

Then Larry recited the details of the third murder.

"The Reverend Donald Pritkin, male, age thirty-eight, father of three, pastor of the Ashland Congregational Church, murdered by same M.O., found in the modest parsonage by his wife when she returned from shopping, Monday, September 6. He was still wearing his golfing clothes."

I looked questioningly for the connection between this pastor and Shannon Perry. "She attended a friend's wedding at that church a few months ago," Larry said. "Reverend Pritkin officiated."

I made a face and shrugged, looking at Earl. He cocked his head as if he agreed that this one was a long shot. That angered Larry. "I didn't say some of these weren't a little farfetched, did I?" he said, almost shouting. "But you can imagine how this girl feels!"

Earl raised a calming hand again, and I wished I hadn't made the face. Larry looked disgusted with both of us, but after a minute he turned back to the wall. "Dale Jerome," he began, and I could hardly believe it. "Male, forty-one, LaSalle Street lawyer, divorced, living alone on Lake Shore Drive, discovered murdered, Wednesday, September 22, same M.O., by landlord when his office called, concerned because he had missed an appointment with a client's corporation counsel."

Larry paused as if in thought. "Several years ago, when Shannon first started working in Chicago, the editor of the paper she wrote for recommended Dale Jerome to her to defend her against a suit filed by the other driver in a minor auto accident. He handled the whole thing with the insurance companies, it never went to court, she only met with him once, and that was it. But she remembered his name, and like any of us when we hear news about someone we've had any contact with before, she said, 'I know that guy!'"

"A lot of people knew *that* guy," I said, trying not to sound too disparaging. "Even back when he represented her on that little case, he was handling big publishing firms and other corporations. It's not unusual that he would have many, many acquaintances."

"I know that, Philip," Larry said, more patiently than before. "But putting it into this context, I mean in light of the fact that she had some contact with each victim, makes it even more significant, wouldn't you say?"

"I suppose," I said, not entirely convinced. Yet.

Wearily, Larry turned back to the board. "Victim number five," he said. "Frances Downs, female, twenty-six, local TV producer, discovered by a friend in her Sandburg Village high rise, Saturday, October 16."

"This is one that puzzles me," Earl interrupted. "This girl was living beyond her means."

"TV producers make good money, don't they?" I said.

"And she was single. No family expenses."

"Yeah, but she wasn't making nearly enough to afford a penthouse in that building. We're talking big bucks here."

"OK," Larry said, "so she may have been a kept woman. We can investigate the rest of her past after Philip gets rolling with Festschrift, but for now I'm interested in the fact that this is another acquaintance of Shannon's."

It was getting very late, and I was tired. But the newspaper clippings of the sixth murder hadn't even yellowed on Earl's wall yet. Two days before, on Wednesday, November 10, Thomas McDough, a forty-eight-year-old dentist, was discovered murdered, apparently by the Thank-You Shooter, in his Marina City Tower condominium. Dr. McDough, a married man whose children were grown and gone, was found by his wife when she returned from an overnight trip. He was Shannon Perry's dentist.

I had to admit it was eerie. Individually, the fact that Shannon Perry knew each victim wasn't much more of a coincidence than that Larry knew number five, Frances Downs. They had been in similar occupations. Earl admitted that he had known the lawyer, Dale Jerome. "At least I knew who he was. His name was familiar to me."

I knew none of them, had not heard of even one of them. But then I had not been a Chicagoan for long. Margo had not mentioned having been familiar with any of the victims either. To know or to at least have had some contact with all six? It was a boggler. I wondered how Larry learned about it.

"She told me," he explained. "I see her every now and then when I visit the old haunts. She's always cheerful and has often asked me to join her at her desk for lunch. But the last few times I've seen her, she's been different. Preoccupied."

"Like you tonight," I suggested.

"Yeah," he admitted, smiling. "I guess. Anyway, I asked her if anything was wrong, and she said maybe she'd tell me about it sometime. I never put it together with the fact that each time I saw her, another murder or two had been committed and that each one cut her deeply because of the name recognition thing every time it came over the newswire. You know, because of her position, she was learning of these murders before anyone else. It got to the point, she told me yesterday, where she dreaded hearing about another murder, wondering what acquaintance or friend would be dead this time."

"How did she finally decide to tell you?"

"Well, I was in to see Chuck Childers, the morning man over there?"

"Yeah."

"And when I went past Shannon's office she didn't even look up. Well, she never misses a thing, so on the way back, I went slowly past her window and made a face, and even though I know she saw me, she didn't respond. So I just walked right in and asked her what was up. She was really distraught. Her boss had told her that her work was suffering for some reason. She's been an award winner for years, but now she can't meet deadlines, misses facts, and all the rest. He wanted her to take a couple of weeks off with pay. She was humiliated—at least that's what I thought."

"She wasn't?"

"I suppose that was part of it, but that wasn't what was

bothering her. She said she had not been able to tell anyone what was bothering her, and that she had been hoping
I might come around because she felt somehow she could
trust me and she knew I am a private detective now. That
got my interest and I assured her she *could* tell me. She
closed the door and burst into tears. I'm tellin' ya, it took
forever to drag it out of her, and I had to promise the
moon, not to mention protecting her confidence. When it
was all over she asked if I would tell her boss, another old
friend of mine, that she was taking him up on the offer of
a couple of weeks off, that she was grateful, and that she
would be back. And I took her home."

"What do you make of it, Larry?" I said. "It's too much
of a long shot to be coincidence I admit. Is this a dangerous
or sick person?"

"Dangerous, no. Sick, possibly. I'd be sick to if it happened to me, wouldn't you?"

I nodded.

"The thing is," he continued, "Shannon has airtight alibis for several of the murders, at least for the ones during
which she can remember where she was, like the most recent ones. I got those out of her by asking the most round-
about questions you've ever heard. The last thing I wanted
to do was to make her think that I thought there was any
possibility she could have been involved. When I had the
alibis all sorted out in my mind, I recounted them to her
to assure her that no second personality or darker side of
her could have committed murders she didn't know about.
She demanded to know then who would be murdering
people to get at her, as if I would know."

"But she was right of course," Earl said. "If she didn't
commit the murders, we're agreed that there are too
many coincidences here for this to be other than deliber-

ate on someone's part. Someone is either trying to frame her or is leading up to threatening her life."

"Of course," Larry said, "but I couldn't tell her that, could I?"

# THREE

Margo's first question at our hastily called Saturday staff meeting the next morning was directed at Larry. "Do we know the floor plans of the murder scenes—I mean of the entire apartment, condo, or house in each instance?"

"We can get them from Festschrift, I assume," Larry said, "but if you don't mind my saying so, that wasn't the first thing I expected to hear from you."

Margo looked puzzled.

"Me either," Earl said.

"All right," she said. "What was I supposed to say?"

"I thought you'd challenge our plan to break her confidence," Larry said.

"Oh, no, I don't think so," Margo said. "You're doing exactly the right thing, and I'm sure that down deep it's what Shannon wants too. She has sworn you to secrecy, Ship, but you've shown her that her worst fear is unfounded: the fear that she has been involved in the murders without knowing it."

"But she doesn't want anyone to know that she's had knowledge—limited though it may be—of every victim," Larry said.

"No, she doesn't want the public to know. But why do you think she told *you?* It's not just because you're a trusted friend, because, let's face it, you really haven't been that close. She wants protection. She has to know, whether she admits it or not, that you're going to feel responsibility for her safety. And don't you?"

"Yeah, I should say I do."

"Then don't feel guilty about your plan to at least tell Festschrift. Even if she insists that no one else know, at least it will give *him* a place to start. You know her name is going to come up in this thing eventually anyway. I assume Chicago Homicide is checking into every member of the Congregational church and will try to round up guest books from all the weddings there in the last year. You know she'll be on some kind of client list of that lawyer's, even though he won her case for her and she may not be thought worth questioning unless everything else fizzles. The dentist's patient list is being scrutinized now, and she'll be more recent and prominent on that one than on any of the others. I don't know how they'll connect her with the Filipino or the Italian woman, but when her name turns up in connection with even two of the others, she'll be under a magnifying glass."

Somehow Margo had summarized what we'd all been toying with since Larry gave the rundown. "You're becoming quite a detective," Earl said. "It makes me wonder why you want to know about the layouts of the murder scenes."

"It's the dish towel part of the M.O. We're pretty confident, because of the absence of unfamiliar fingerprints at each scene, that the murderer was wearing gloves. And based on the careful digging and scraping to remove the slug, the tidy cleanup work, and the placing of the shell in the victim's hand, we can guess that the murderer was wearing small, thin gloves, maybe even rubber or surgical ones. Those would frighten someone, however. No one would let someone in wearing surgical gloves. So we can guess that the murderer was wearing regular gloves over rubber gloves upon entering the house or apartment."

"I'm with you so far," Earl said, "but I confess I don't know where you're going."

"Who wears gloves at this time of year?" Margo asked.

"Certainly not men for the most part."

"Handymen might," Larry said. "Maybe repairmen, maintenance men, garbagemen."

"Well, that's true," Margo said, appearing to resign from whatever hypothesis she had been building.

"But what does that have to do with the layout of the scenes?" Earl asked again.

"Well, I was thinking I was on a track that might make us lean toward a female perpetrator," Margo said. "I don't guess the gloves angle is exclusive to women after all. But I was hoping to put that together with the fact that the murderer always soiled a dish towel in sopping up the blood."

"Keep going," Larry said.

"Never a bathroom towel," Margo said, "never a rag from under the sink or anything else lying around? What does that say to you? Anything?"

"So what you want to know," Earl said, "is whether any of the murders occurred closer to the bathroom than to the kitchen, and if so, why did the murderer use a dish towel rather than something handier."

"Exactly."

"Good question. I'm not sure it's necessarily a feminine thing to choose a dish towel over something else, but it could be. It could also just be part of the sick pattern here."

"If so, it would have no significance," Margo said.

"Right, but let's check it out if I can hook Philip up with Wally."

We were all eager to know what our various assignments would be on this most important case—assigned from a higher level than ever, too. Earl started by having us call every client on our active cases list and inform them that their investigation was being either canceled, postponed, or reassigned to another company. It was our job to pacify them without giving them any reasons. In some cases we would refund a major portion if not all of their fee, even if the case was being reassigned.

When Larry and Earl were finished with their calls they split up for separate trips to Chicago, Larry to tell Shannon what he wanted to do about her problem, and Earl to sell Wally Festschrift on his idea for me. I called Bonnie.

"Earl asked if you could contact the agency that runs the building for him and see how long that vacant apartment will be open," I told her. "He'd like to have it available for agency use for the next month or so, at least until December 15."

After lunch Margo and I drove up to Highland Park to a mostly deserted playground. A few kids played softball with their coats on, and we smelled charcoaled burgers and hot dogs as we strolled. "Earl has been so close," Margo said. "I hope working with Sergeant Festschrift again will be a good thing for him."

She was talking about Earl's interest in God. Ever since we had known him, Margo and I had struggled with just how to tell him what Christ meant to us and that we had found Him to be a personal God. Earl had gone from amusement with us to hostility to reluctant listening, and then to a roller coaster of reactions that seemed to depend on his moods or what was happening in his life at the moment.

We had decided on a moratorium on overt selling and just prayed that somehow God would use us to show Earl what we had been unable to tell him. It was amazing just to think of all the people—even non-Christians—whose advice we sought for how to share the most important thing in life with someone we cared about. Someone I asked told me, "The very phrase 'share with someone' has a religious ring to it that'll turn him off."

For a while we were uncertain about the effectiveness of our new resolve to do more living of the faith in front of Earl than preaching it to him. He seemed to enjoy the truce. It's not that we had ever put him on the spot or challenged him, but I confess I had frequently spiritualized things and had unintentionally come off seeming "holier than thou." For a while it seemed all I did was ask for chances to tell the staff all about Christ. When he finally relented, I didn't feel I had done well, though no one seemed offended.

We wanted so badly to see those people we loved come to Christ. But again, there was that terminology so foreign to them. The strangest break came, however, when Earl's old friend, Wally Festschrift, reappeared out of the past.

Oh he had been there all the time, but the men had basically lost touch over the years. It wasn't just that Earl had worked for Wally when he first became a cop, but as Earl rose quickly through the ranks, he passed Wally and for a time Wally wound up working for Earl. And did Wally give Earl fits then.

Maybe it was jealousy. Wally denies it. Maybe he really was—as he claims now—trying to make Earl a better cop. Maybe he hated to see the department lose Earl; Wally says he saw it coming two years before it happened. "He was too smooth, too good; you just knew somebody in politics was gonna snap him up. I just didn't want him to get too big for his britches before he left us. Yeah I gave 'im a hard time. So what?"

A hard time was understating it to hear Earl tell it. He says Wally was the toughest guy to supervise in all of Homicide. "I mean, there's something going on when a guy is in the same position, sergeant in Homicide, for fifteen years, and that's after several years as a homicide detective."

Wally explained that it simply was and always will be his first love. The mystery, the people, and most of all, as he once told me, the sense of justice when the heat finally comes down on the guilty.

I liked Festschrift, though he took some getting used to. First impressions are always worse, especially when it comes to Wally. But regardless of how interesting he was—and how excited I was at the prospect of working closely with him again on this new scheme of Earl's—the most important thing was that Wally and Earl had not just made up for their past squabbles. They had developed a new relationship.

Wally is divorced and his kids have turned out bad. He is a lonely old cop. Earl is a young widower whose only child is an institutionalized autistic who has never recognized his father. Neither would admit his loneliness, though Festschrift once confessed to me his failure as a husband and father.

But you should have seen it when they were reunited on a case that happened to overlap Chicago Homicide with the EH Detective Agency. At first there was formality, cautious sparring, maneuvering, diplomacy, politics, a few flare-ups, and territorial scuffles. But then they realized they needed each other, and the old professionalism and camaraderie of the fraternity of cops took over and they were old war buddies again. It was exciting, not to mention educational, just to hear them reminisce about some of the old cases. That was when Festschrift finally tried to explain away his despicable performance as a subordinate. It was not as a cop, mind you, that Wally was hard to take. Earl used to always concede that. In a boss/employee relationship, Wally was nearly impossible to deal with. Wally had been a good boss, Earl said, but he made a lousy subordinate.

"It wasn't jealousy, no matter what you say or what you think," Wally said a dozen times during the Johnny Bizell murder case which brought the two back together. "I was just the stone that polished you into what you are today." Whereupon Earl would swear and then excuse himself.

Somewhere during that renewed relationship, Earl started telling Wally Festschrift about Christ. I know what you're thinking. You're thinking you missed something, that I forgot to tell you when Earl's mind and heart got changed and he became receptive and prayed to become a Christian. But he didn't. I'm saying the man started telling his friend that Christ could forgive his past and could give him a new and abundant life, and Earl hadn't even dipped into the gift for himself yet.

"And he still hasn't," Margo said, as we walked in the park.

"No, but remember when he said he'd noticed that we'd been strangely silent about these kinds of things for a while and that made us ashamed of our strategy?"

"Yeah," she said, "but in reality I think the strategy had a lot to do with it. He started asking more questions on his own, and we were able to answer without feeling as if we were shoving anything down his throat. For as classy a guy as Earl is, he's also proud, and he's not about to be sold a bill of goods or be badgered into anything."

"That's for sure," I said. "I've seen him with more than

one can't-miss salesman who missed. Remember when he told the one that he wasn't motivated by great amounts of money?"

Margo nodded and laughed. "Where was the poor guy supposed to go from there? He told Earl he could donate the profits to his favorite charity and Earl said, 'You're looking at it.'"

We watched the kids play ball for a while, and Margo grew serious. "I also remember when Earl came to us after he had started talking to Wally and told us that all he could remember about how to receive Christ was that you just pray, confess your sins, and believe. He knew there had to be more to it than that, so he wanted a little counsel before he headed back out to his little mission field."

It had been a shocking revelation to us. Here was Earl, "sharing" a faith he didn't have, doing the work we should have been doing, and yet not afraid to ask us for input. He also made clear that night that he had all the information he needed to make his own decision about it, and so he expected to be left alone to make it. We got the point, but that didn't make it any easier over the ensuing months.

The Bizell case was solved. Earl continued to talk with Wally occasionally, but they eventually drifted apart—that's what the thirty miles between the Loop and the North Shore will do to you—and as far as we knew, neither of them made a commitment. We tested the waters with Earl a few times, but he just reminded us that we had done our part and the rest was up to him.

That didn't stop us from praying, of course, and we found ourselves doing that more than ever. "It's what we should have been doing all along," Margo said, "instead of talking so much."

She's always been hard to argue with, especially when she's right.

We leaned against a huge tree and pulled our coat collars up higher around our necks. Her full, brown hair waved in the wind, and she hunched her shoulders to keep warm. I had been struck by her beauty long before I fell in love with her. I had been so involved in her personal problems that I assumed anything I felt for her was merely pity. And when I realized otherwise, it was hard to convince *her* it wasn't pity.

But over the few years, through all the rough times we'd seen, even through our brief breakup not long before, I had loved her. And I had seen her grow. Better than that, she had seen *me* grow.

If she hadn't, we wouldn't have been standing there in the park, looking deep into each other's eyes. Her smile always reached me. I loved her. I loved her before I knew it. I loved her when I thought I didn't. I loved her before she loved me. I loved her when I was certain she didn't love me anymore, and when she had reason not to. We loved each other now, and regardless of what would happen to her love in the future, mine would never waver again.

"I never quit loving you," she said softly. "Even if I acted like it. Even if I thought you didn't deserve it."

"I didn't . . ." I said, but she put a finger to my lips.

"I was hopelessly in love with you even when I thought I had lost you to someone else just because I had asked for some time. I was willing to give you up if that's what was meant to be, but I can't imagine what my life would have been without you."

I loved to hear her talk like that, but saying so would only have spoiled it. I reached over to her face and slipped my fingers between her hair and her neck and pulled her face to mine. As we kissed, two little boys giggled and pointed. Margo turned and winked at them. Then she embraced me.

# FOUR

By the time I entered our office Monday morning, more things had been set in motion than I had even known were planned. I got in late Sunday night and was unaware that Earl and Larry had moved Shannon Perry into the vacant apartment at the end of the hall.

Earl had also arranged for me to meet with Sergeant Wally Festschrift at the precinct house downtown and had somehow talked Wally into tutoring me for the duration of the Thank-You Shooter investigation.

Bonnie was filling me in at our front desk. "Does this mean I'm not going to get to meet Shannon before I hook up with Wally?"

Before she could answer, Earl poked his head out and asked Margo and me to join him and Larry in his office. "There's someone I'd like you to meet," he said.

Margo straightened her desk and caught up with me. When we entered Earl's office, a young woman of about twenty-five stood and extended her hand. Medium height and slender, Shannon Perry was a pretty girl with short-cropped, dark brown hair, bright blue eyes, and a gleaming though tentative smile. She wore a pale pink blouse with a contrasting burgundy ribbon tied in a bow at the neck and a cream-colored crocheted vest and a leather belt over a light gray, pleated skirt. Signs of her trauma became evident as we talked. Earl had a couple of extra chairs dragged in, then filled us in on the arrangements he and Larry had made with Shannon.

"You were right, Margo," he began. "Shannon's real desire is for protection. As far as we can tell, no one knows she's here. She'll stay with us for the entire two weeks she has off, unless she comes under suspicion by the Chicago P.D.; then we'd have to inform them of her whereabouts. Meanwhile, while Philip is working with Wally downtown, we'll be asking Shannon about everyone in her life to see what the story is."

"I don't look forward to that," Shannon said quietly, "but I know I've had enough of this torture. That's why I really didn't mind when Larry told me he had confided in all of you. I think if he had not assured me that you can help and that you are all convinced I am innocent, I wouldn't have felt good about you knowing. I'm still not sure why you want to make this contact with the Chicago police sergeant."

Overarticulate is the only way to describe Shannon's precise, cultured speech. She had a way of saying exactly what she meant.

"We feel it's a real break," Earl said. "We'll have access to information, and Sergeant Festschrift will have our input in a nonthreatening way. And maybe we can get a good bead on the murderer."

Shannon nodded but didn't speak.

"You know," Larry said, "we are pretty certain that the murderer is someone you know well, Shannon."

"That's scary," she said. "What does it all mean? Is someone trying to frame me?"

"I don't think so," Earl said. "The advertising on the shells has nothing to do with you, does it? Is overpoliteness one of your hang-ups, or do you know someone with the initials *S.D.?*"

"No. In fact, when I heard of the first murder, of that young man in my neighborhood, I assumed the murderer was someone who wanted to be caught. This fastidiousness at the crime scene and the message and initials on the bullet just seemed like the work of someone who was crying out for help or at least someone who wants to be caught."

"That could still be true," Margo said. "But with five more murders and no more clues, I'm beginning to wonder."

"There's something I feel guilty about," Shannon said. "We all know there are literally hundreds of Chicago policemen combing the city right now, looking for clues, interviewing door-to-door in the neighborhoods where the murders took place. They even questioned me after the Ng murder simply because I live close by. If you're convinced the murderer is someone who knows me, shouldn't we help the police focus their search a little better?"

Earl stood. "That's what I've been wanting to hear," he said. "We were worried about your request for secrecy. You know if we tell the Chicago P.D., they'll probably take the case right out of our hands. It will be difficult to keep your name out of the news. My fear is that when this leaks out, and you know it will if very many people know about it, it'll scare the murderer out of the city and we'll never be able to track him down."

"Or her," Margo said, and Shannon flinched.

"Her?"

"Very possibly," Margo said, looking directly at Shannon. "I would start this investigation with your girlfriends, your co-workers, even your relatives. Someone who knows you very, very well is killing people who are a relatively small part of your life. It's almost as if it is someone with access to your records, your datebook, your wallet, or something."

"We've got a problem," Larry said ominously. "If Shannon was interviewed after the Ng murder in June, she's on file. And when that dentist's client list is cross-referenced by computer with all the names associated with the other murders, it's going to spit her name right out."

Earl grimaced. "You're right of course. Let's see, is there any way that she could be associated with any of the other victims, officially I mean? I can't see how they could associate her with the Matacena woman. And it would be ages before she would be placed at a wedding officiated by Pritkin. Did you go alone to that wedding, Shannon?"

"No. In fact I had a date and a bunch of us went together from work."

"Who was your date?"

"Jake," she said.

"Jake Raven?" Larry said. "Your boss?"

"Yes. You know Jake."

"I don't know him like I know Chuck—"

"Childers?"

"Uh-huh, but we all used to hang around together in the old days."

"It wasn't that long ago, Larry," Shannon said.

"Yeah I know. Just seems like it."

"We're getting off my point, Lar," Earl said. "The fact that several people from W . . ."

"MTR-FM," Shannon offered.

"Yeah, went with you to this wedding must mean that

several people from work also remembered it when the murder was revealed."

"Yes, we talked about it."

"Well, let's take this slowly then," Margo said. "I see what Earl is getting at. The odds are that, since the Ng murder was the first, and it did just seem interesting at that point for it to have happened in your neighborhood, Shannon, you had no reason not to talk about it with your friends. It was normal to discuss how spooky it was to have something like that happen on your street, in your block. You must've talked about staying with someone for a while and having new locks put in and all that."

"Exactly," Shannon said. Looking first at Larry, then at Earl, she added, "Sometimes Margo seems to know me better than I do," and she leaned over and squeezed Margo's hand to assure her it was a compliment. "As a matter of fact I did stay with Jeanie for a couple of nights, but I never did get new locks. I already had the best you can buy anyway, and the strange thing is that there had been no forced entry into Mr. Ng's place. All the reports said the murderer had to have been someone he trusted. I don't know anyone he knew, at least, not that I am aware of. And I had only spoken with him a time or two, so cautiously I moved back home."

"But Margo's point is that everyone at work was aware of your apartment's proximity to the victim's, right?" Earl said.

Shannon nodded.

"And it's likely you expressed some reaction when the Matacena woman was murdered." Margo's voice was calm and even.

"Oh, yes. I talked about her with some of the people who were with me on that assignment. Since we're a small staff, that includes almost everyone in our office."

Margo began scribbling notes and stood to study the clips on the wall. "Everyone at work knew Frances Downs too, so when she was murdered panic set in. That brought it right downtown and applied it to someone who was more than just a neighbor. Am I right to assume all of you had seen her at various news events and social functions, maybe had lunch with her a time or two?"

"Yes, that's right."

"So the big question is whether everyone in your office knows that you were also acquainted with the lawyer, Jerome, or the dentist, McDough. If they do, then you aren't the only one with a terrible secret. Of course, whoever's murdering these people knows of your acquaintances with them, however limited. But who would know about Jerome and McDough? Somebody else where you work I mean."

"No one I think," Shannon said after a moment. "By the time Mr. Jerome was found murdered, I knew enough not to tell anyone. I may have mentioned him in passing before that, you know, like when his name was in the news for some other reason. I might have told someone at that time that he had helped me once. But when he was murdered I didn't mention it to anyone. I was sick of the coincidences by then."

"And nobody mentioned it, nobody asked you? Not even whoever it might have been that you had mentioned his name to before?"

"No," Shannon said, shaking her head slowly. "No one said anything to me."

"I'm still stuck on your date at the wedding, Shannon," Larry said.

"I told you it was Jake."

"But I don't remember you ever seeing Jake socially."

"Oh I never did, really. I mean, we didn't date like

Chuck and I used to. About that time, I was getting over breaking up with Chuck, and Jake was just doing me a favor. We sat together, that's all. I think we went to dinner once or twice, but his divorce wasn't final and I wasn't comfortable dating a man who was still married."

"His divorce has been final for some time now, but you still don't date him, do you?"

"No, I was never really interested in him, and he knew that. Still, when he was legally married I didn't want to be seen with him in any situation that could look compromising."

"I don't think the guest register from that wedding will be checked for quite some time," Earl said. "But I think we're narrowing the possibilities anyway. We're going to want to get into your relationships with the men at your office some more, but let's cover your reaction to this most recent murder. Who at work knew that McDough was your dentist?"

"I'm not certain. I know I didn't mention it to anyone when it happened. I thought that anyone who happened to know could ask me about it. At that point I didn't want to volunteer any information."

"And no one brought it up?"

"Chuck might have. Or Jake. But I don't remember. Wait. Yes. Jake said something. He asked if that was what was bothering me when he suggested I take a few weeks off. It was just after that that I saw Larry."

"Let me ask this, and then I've gotta go," I said. "Did you feel that anyone at work grew suspicious of you or acted wary of you when they put together the Ng, Matacena, Pritkin, and Downs murders?"

Shannon thought a moment. "No, I don't think so There may have been some mention of the coincidences, but then, you see, almost everyone there had had as much contact with Matacena, Pritkin, and Downs as I had."

"The question I have," Earl said, sitting again, "is why everyone there isn't a little paranoid. Are newspeople so egotistical that they think they routinely come into contact with three people who wind up murdered by the same perpetrator? You started getting a sickening feeling pretty quickly, Shannon, and admittedly, you have some connection with *every* victim. But it seems to me everybody in that office ought to be wondering the same things you are. Is it me? Am I the murderer? Or am I the next victim? Or is it one of my co-workers?"

Shannon appeared almost relieved. "I see what you mean," she said. "I don't know if any of them knew all six, like I did, but even knowing half of them is too much of a coincidence, isn't it?"

"You bet it is," Earl said. "Philip, let me see you before you go."

Earl walked me down to the car where we chatted in the cold wind. "By the time you see Wally he could be onto this girl," he said.

"How do you mean *onto* her, Earl? Do you think she's—?"

"I don't know. Larry is confident of her alibis. We'll check them out more closely later. What I'm saying is that while the three victims everyone else in her office had some contact with will be hard to connect with Shannon or any of the rest of them—except this Downs girl, and they'll all be talked to about that one eventually—Shannon will certainly be linked with Ng and McDough. When they check to see if she was at the Downs funeral, that will make a pretty stark list. It won't take long for them to find her on Jerome's old client list; that had to be only five or six years ago. And when they ask questions of her co-workers, and you know they will at that point, she's going to be quickly matched with every victim."

"But won't her alibis protect her?"

"From conviction, if they're solid. From publicity? This will ruin her life. We're convinced the murderer is someone with something against Shannon. This is either a way to try to frame her—which I doubt—or to scare her to death, or to set up her murder. Frankly, I am afraid whoever has killed all these people plans to kill Shannon. But our first concern is that if Chicago gets onto this soon, and you know they will, we still have to protect Shannon."

"Are you saying we won't tell Chicago we've got her out here?"

"You can tell Festschrift, but we're buying his confidence."

"I don't follow."

"Don't tell him anything until her name comes up. You know it will, Philip. It won't take long. He'll check with her boss and learn that she's off for a couple of weeks, and all of a sudden there's an all-points bulletin—"

"And all of a sudden we're harboring a suspect."

"Yeah, unless you tell Wally quickly enough so that he can take some heat off. If he can protect her privacy, we'll let him come out here and talk to her. We'll give him everything we've got because we're convinced she can lead to the killer if all the noise doesn't scare him or her off."

"And if Wally doesn't mention her name today or tonight?"

"Then you keep your mouth shut. I'll see you later."

I was supposed to meet Wally Festschrift for lunch at 11:30, and I was running late. I didn't know whether to just head straight for his favorite sit-down burger joint or try to catch him at the precinct house. He often ran late for everything except lunch, but I knew he had the smell of blood in his nostrils on this one and might lose himself in the chase. Here was his chance to look good again. It had been a couple of years since he broke a big murder case. Every few months he tracked down a tough one, but even he couldn't deny that there is a certain amount of satisfaction—even if he was immune to pride—in seeing your name in the paper as the one whose hunch or unusual insight led to the capture of some particularly horrifying perpetrator of a heinous crime.

He was the best in the business according to Earl. And Earl should know, because many consider *him* the best. Earl's opinion of Wally is shared by many, including Wally. He admitted it to me once, but I didn't detect an ounce of braggadocio.

"I just flat care," he had said. "Just like the card company on TV that says they care enough to do the very best or something like that."

Apparently Wally doesn't watch enough TV to get the commercials straight, but he was close enough and I knew what he meant. He was careful. He was tireless. He wanted justice. And his car was in the lot at the station.

It was hard to miss. It looked like a renovated taxicab. It was the shade of green painted only on cars bought in fleets. Blackwalled tires, a city license plate, two whip antennae, a spotlight, a bash here and a ding there. This was the most marked unmarked squad car in the city. It had more than a hundred thousand miles on it, rocked when it stopped, and lurched in the turns. You wore a seat belt when you could dig one out, more for safety within the car during normal trips around the city than for some more ominous possibility. This wasn't a car that would ever be junked. It would need to be shot.

Of course Festschrift fit the car. It was his responsibility, so it wasn't as if he were inheriting all those ills. There were things wrong with it that he could have had taken care of and then be reimbursed by the city, but cars weren't his thing. Murders, more specifically *murderers*, were his thing.

When I jogged up the steps of the station house, Wally was coming out of a seminar room with a couple of dozen other plainclothes detectives who were pocketing their notepads. It appeared someone was trying to tell him a joke, and he was pretending to guffaw—too early, of course—while continuing to scribble notes on the backs of several of his business cards with a stubby pencil.

The joke-teller turned away shaking his head as Wally absently slowed to a stop in the middle of the lobby, unknowingly forcing everyone in the area to detour around his massive body.

His greasy hair, which was either cut very short or was in need of cutting depending on when you caught him—right now it needed to be cut, probably because he'd been putting in fourteen-hour days—hung in strands over his ears. His bald spot was visible as he bowed to make his final note. I stood by the door, waiting for him to notice me on his way out.

He was a sight. His meaty hands stuffed the business cards into his wallet, which he then jammed in his hip pocket. "Can't stand those big things makin' yer jacket hang sideways," he muttered. With his big trench coat in a ball under one arm, he unbuttoned his green suit jacket, hiked up his pants, and went through contortions to tuck in his white shirt which was suffering from a bad case of gapsiosis. I expected at any minute to see the buttons pop off one by one. His tie was at least six inches too short. Pulling his pants up over his belly exposed his sensible shoes, the kind with thick rubber soles. And of course, he was wearing white socks, the trademark of detectives who have been detectives through several decades and never bothered to notice the changes in fashion.

Dragging the trench coat on, but making no attempt to button it, the big man finally started moving toward the door. As if he had known I was standing there all along, he threw his arm around me without seeming to even look at me and said, "Philip, my boy, welcome to Chicago Homicide, where we do it right. Wait till I tell you what we just learned from the fancy-schmantzy psychologist."

# FIVE

"The regular, but make it two," Wally told the waiter as we sat at a table in his kind of restaurant.

"One for each?" asked the man behind the counter.

"Ah, no," Wally said. "Philip, you want what I'm havin'?"

"Sure, why not?"

"OK, Julio, make that three regulars."

Wally peeled off both his topcoat and his suit jacket and piled them on an empty chair. "Very interesting," he said. "Really. Here, let me show you. I love this psychology stuff, I really do. I think if that poor Dr. Shrink-woman ever saw a murder scene she'd be packin' for Podunk. But she does seem to know her stuff, and some of my own research bears her out."

Wally waited to see if I thought that sounded funny. It did, but I wasn't going to laugh at him. When I didn't, he did. "I'm dead serious." He said it with a twinkle, but I knew he was.

He dug into his hip pocket for the wallet, almost having to stand to get to it, and produced the batch of cards on which he had recorded an hour's lecture on the potential characteristics of the Thank-You Shooter based on the computerized evidence Homicide had presented to the psychologist.

"Look at this," he began, leaning forward and showing me the back of one of the cards. I wouldn't have been able to read one word of it if my life depended on it, but I nodded as if I could read all the words. "She says they're pretty sure this murderer is actually committing mass suicide, killing his or her own personality or alter ego."

I cocked my head, not knowing what I thought of that and certainly not knowing what Wally thought of it.

"Either way, it's interesting, isn't it?" he said.

"Yeah, I'll grant you that. But how did she come up with a theory like that?"

"Well, you know we've been interviewing everyone connected with all the victims, except this dentist, of course, 'cause that just happened and we're still tryin' to get a bead on everyone in his sphere. I like that word *sphere*, don't you?"

I nodded. It wasn't one of my favorites, but I was willing to like whatever Wally liked.

"It makes me sound like a shrink, doesn't it?"

I nodded again.

"But what I'm gettin' at," he continued, "or what she was gettin' at anyway, and I tend to agree with her, is that there is indeed a pattern with these victims." I nearly jumped, but it wasn't what I had thought. "I mean, we still don't know if the murderer is male or female. Lots of us have different views on that."

"What's yours?"

"It's irrelevant at this point, Philip," he said. "Which is a nice way of saying that I don't have the foggiest and I'm not sure it would help me if I did. Knowing the sex of the murderer will become very important as we start closing the net, of course, because you'll cut off half your prospects, which is a nice trim if you can get it. Know what I mean?"

I wasn't sure I did, but I nodded anyway. And our food was delivered. Mercy. His *regular* was a half-pound burger and a mountain of cottage fries with a Coke in a milk shake tin. He had two of everything. One of each was going to be more than enough for me. Still he would finish first, even while carrying the bulk of the conversation (no pun intended).

"The point is this," he said, depositing a quarter of the burger into one cheek as if storing it for the winter—amazingly, it didn't affect his speech in the least; it was as if his mouth was still empty—"a pattern of types among the victims is important in getting a bead on the murderer, right?"

"Sure." I wasn't, but it sounded good.

"OK. I don't mind tellin' ya, this case has had me buffaloed all this time. It drives me nuts that this guy, or girl, or whatever, is still out there when there are such obvious clues being left at each scene. I know the guy—and let me call him or her that for the sake of briefery or whatever they call it—is going to make a mistake one of these times and give himself away, but see, my goal is to nail him *before* the next one, not after. We just can't let another murder happen. I was hurt bad by this dentist buyin' it because even though we didn't have much of a lead on the killer, I thought we were making enough racket that we could scare him off for a while. Apparently I was wrong, and it's gonna take more than what we had to either flush him out or keep him down for a while. If we can just keep him quiet for a while, we can get him without his killing anyone else. I got some associates who want him to kill a few more people just so we'll maybe get more clues. That's sick. Don't you agree that's sick?"

That was not hard at all to agree with. I was getting a little impatient. "So, what's the pattern among the victims? Whatever it is, it hasn't come out in what we read in the papers, because we can't seem to put anything together." I wasn't lying. We hadn't put Shannon together with the victims. Shannon had. From what we knew, we had drawn a blank.

"Oh, and I just know ol' Earl is a-studying those clippings, even though he knows better. We're not giving the papers everything we've got, though I must admit we don't have much more than you read. But I never knew of anyone solving a murder by reading the papers."

Wally had finished one of the Cokes and a burger and was polishing off the last of the first mess of fries. He didn't appear to be slowing down. "There *is* a common denominator among these victims," he said. I knew that, but I hadn't thought he did. Luckily, his was different from mine.

"Let me give you some basics of what we've found and see if you don't come to the same conclusions," he said. "I'll take them in order: Ng, Matacena, Pritkin, Jerome, Downs, and McDough." He did that without notes. The details of this case had long since been burned into his brain. He noticed my awe of the recital. "I haven't been on another case since the second murder," he said.

"Now, about Ng. He's one of these quiet types. Doesn't have trouble with the language, but is still shy, almost as if he does. He's detail-oriented, an organizer, a super-athlete type. Likes to get the kids of the neighborhood involved in the Park District programs. But here's the thing that sets him apart, aside from being kind of a shy loner. Nobody really knows him well. He keeps to himself basically, at least in relation to adults. Never dates. Was never married. But spends lots of time with kids. "Never brings them home. His landlady said she never saw any kids at his place, but said he seemed to work long hours. His boss verified that. He was salaried, no overtime pay, but worked long days. Maybe because he had nothing and no one else. But anyway, his boss also said that in spite of his modest salary, he had put kids in programs who couldn't pay the fees and somehow the fees got paid. The boss knew Lawson was paying. Now what does that tell you?"

Wally took me by surprise. I wasn't sure it told me anything. I was enjoying hearing him wrap up the information he had gathered. "I didn't know there was gonna be a test," I said, smiling weakly.

"Well, there is. What does that tell you? What do you know about Ng based on what I told you? We've gotta know the victims if we're ever gonna know the murderer."

He took a long drink of his second Coke, never taking his eyes off me. I felt as if I were in the hot seat. I would hate to be a suspect he's interrogating. "He's a nice guy," I tried, "a loner. Organized?"

"C'mon," he said. "You can do better'n that. Anybody can figure that out. His friends and neighbors knew that before he got snuffed. What do you know about him that's not so much on the surface, something we might put together with another victim that would make a pattern?"

"He's sympathetic to the down-and-outers?" I asked.

"That's it!" he said, using his burger bun to sop up the catsup from his fries. "It ain't big, I'll admit, but keep that in your head as you hear about the rest of the victims." He stood heavily and peeled a ten from his wallet and began the process of putting all those coats back on. He stuck the receipt into his shirt pocket as we left and loudly bid farewell to every noncustomer in the place. They all smiled blank, uncomprehending smiles in wonder at the man who ate big, tipped big, and always ordered the same. They didn't understand much of his English, but they liked him and he liked them.

"Good place, huh?" he said, squeezing behind the wheel of the Festschriftmobile.

I was stuffed, almost miserable. "Yeah," I managed. "Good place. Thanks."

"Thank the City of Chicago, brother. I'm on duty and you're—what does Earl call it—an intern?"

"Yeah."

"Yeah, an intern. Sounds good. Anyway, you wanna hear about victim number two?"

"Sure."

"'Course ya do. Annamarie Matacena," he announced in an Italian dialect. "Another quiet foreigner. At work she keeps to herself. She's quiet. To her, language *is* a barrier. She's a sad woman with a tough life. She's never gotten over her divorce, and money is always tight. She makes so little that her food and rent are subsidized. She's a hard worker, not lazy. Not quick or ambitious, but a self-starter. She's never in the way but always there when you need her. What would you guess she's like at home?"

"Same as Ng," I said, wondering why Wally always spoke of the victims in the present tense, as if they were still alive.

"Not a bad guess. It was my guess too. If you get any comfort out of being just as wrong as the best homicide cop in the city, welcome. Even though this woman is fifty-one years old, she's got a daughter and two grandkids living with her, plus a couple of more grandkids from a no-good son who ran out on his wife. Are you ready for this? She also takes care of a couple of Mexican kids in the neighborhood.

"Now, Philip, it's one thing for a woman with an ethnic background that is big in family relationships to take care of her own and be embarrassed by divorce and a son gone bad, but to take in other kids, not her own and not even her own nationality. What have we got here?"

"Another Ng?"

"You got it. The woman cares about the down-and-outer. She's got nothing to live on, but she's got plenty of company helping her live on it. But the quiet, out-of-the-way, keep-to-herself type at home? Nope. We were both wrong on that. She is loud, an intruder in neighborhood politics. She screams at her family, all of 'em, her own and the borrowed ones. They fight long and hard and at the top of their lungs, but they are fiercely loyal to each other and watch out for each other."

"So Ng and Matacena are sympathetic to the underprivileged," I said. "And Matacena is underprivileged herself. What does that tell you?"

"I'm the teacher here, kid. And it doesn't tell us anything, yet. Let's talk about the third victim, the preacher. Beautiful family. Loved by the congregation. Not all preachers can say that, ya know. Anyway, if he had a fault, it was that he went above and beyond the call of duty. I know these guys are supposed to have a higher calling anyway, and you might think that because he was golfing on his day off—that Monday—that he was a typical suburban pastor, kinda affluent, a country-club type. Fact is, he was a duffer. Had only taken up golf in the past few months. Used second-hand shoes and borrowed clubs. His wife said he rarely took his whole day off. He might shoot a round of golf or go fishing, but he liked to be home when the kids got home from school so he could play with them in the yard or go bike riding or something. But Monday nights he was downtown doing volunteer work with the Salvation Army. Can you beat that?"

"That *is* hard to believe. Puts him in the sympathetic category again, doesn't it?"

"So, why is someone killing off nice guys, especially in light of what the shrink told us today? Is the murderer a nice guy who doesn't want to be nice? Maybe he'd rather speak his mind, stick up for himself, do something for himself once, but he's weak. He hates the nice guy in him because the nice guy isn't really nice. He just gets walked on. He does what people ask."

"Interesting."

"Uh-huh." Wally fell silent, carefully picking his way through Loop traffic on his way to South LaSalle Street. Cabs and small trucks that attempted to cut him off didn't get far, and when they got a good look at the car they backed off. At a city-owned parking garage that would have charged the price of our lunch to park for more than an hour, he wiggled from behind the wheel, deftly flashed his badge, and we headed down the street to a tall office building.

He mashed a button on the elevator and said, "I live with these victims every day, Philip. I mean I know them better now than I would've if I'd been their friend. It's because I know everyone who knew them. I know who liked 'em, who didn't, who they liked and who they didn't, who they worked for and who worked for them. Friends don't have that kinda perspective, but I do. I know when they got up in the morning and when they went to bed at night. I think about 'em, eat with 'em, dream about 'em."

"Don't you ever get tired of it?"

"Tired of them, maybe, but not tired of *it*, because *it* is all there is. *It* is what I am, kid. *It* is the search, the trail, the puzzle, the game. My boss doesn't like to hear me call it a game, and somehow, now that I'm older and more mature than when I was givin' your boss fits, I know what he means. When it's the murderer of some scum bag or socialite who never gave a thought to anyone else anyway, only the justice and the mystery keep me going, because regardless of the quality of the life that was taken, it shouldn't have been taken. And it's my job to deliver the guilty party to the people. But when it's a mass murder of decent people and when the poor jerk pulling these jobs is leaving us clues and begging us to catch him, then I gotta agree, it's more than a game. No, I never get tired of it."

We exited left off the elevator and padded down a dimly lit, carpeted hallway past a security guard who hardly looked at Festschrift's badge. We pushed open a huge mahogany door with a half dozen names painted in gold on it and found ourselves in a waiting room with three couches and several large wing chairs. The receptionist sat behind a great dark desk that would have been appropriate in a corporation president's office.

"Chicago Homicide," Festschrift said softly, showing his badge. "We'd like to talk with the secretary to the late Mr. Jerome."

"Hello, Sergeant," the receptionist said. "I assume you're aware that you're not the first to see Miss Severinsen this week—in fact you're the fifth or sixth. And I believe you've been here a couple of times before."

"Oh yeah?" Festschrift said unimpressed. "Is she complaining about that or are you the only one around here who doesn't care if we find out who did it?"

It was cold, but it was beautiful, and the receptionist pushed a button. "Miss Severinsen?"

"Yes?"

"A policeman is here to see you."

As she escorted us to the inner office, the receptionist said, "I know you've got your job to do, but I can't imagine there's any more the poor woman can tell you. You just caught her, you know. Within the hour she'll be gone. She's leaving."

"Oh?"

"Yes, the gentleman who's replacing Mr. Jerome brought his own secretary and, rather than take another position with us, Miss Severinsen is moving to another firm."

The slender, graying, middle-aged secretary was teary-eyed as we entered. Festschrift introduced me as his associate. She was taping the top of a box, but she offered us chairs and then sat down herself. "Is there anything I can tell you today that I didn't tell you the last time, Sergeant?" she said, not unkindly.

"Probably not," Wally said, more compassionately than I had ever heard him. In spite of his appearance, he could be gentle when he wanted to. All as a means to an end, admittedly, but then perhaps there was more real sympathy in there than I thought. "I know this is terribly difficult for you and that you were very close to Mr. Jerome. Basically I just wanted to come by and wish you the best in your new job and to tell you that I would be thinking of you and hoping that it will in some small way help take your mind off this difficult memory."

Miss Severinsen dabbed at her eyes. "Well thank you so much. I'm looking forward to it, under the circumstances."

There was an awkward silence as she apparently wondered if that were really all Festschrift had come for. "You could do me one little favor," he said finally, and I detected a slight stiffening in her. "It might be the easiest question I've ever asked you about Mr. Jerome." She appeared willing to hear the question at least, but she said nothing. "You've told me that he was basically a kind and generous man and that he was excellent in his profession. But could you tell me anything else that would help me get a picture of his personality—something in the area of selflessness or helping the little guy. Everybody knows these high-powered lawyers have lots of money and influence, so it's kind of easy for them to appear gracious and humanitarian. But I get the impression from you that he was genuine in his concern for the down-and-outer."

"Well, maybe not the real down-and-outer, because, as you may know, there isn't too much that a lawyer of Mr. Jerome's stature can do for a truly disadvantaged person. But yes, there were people he helped who couldn't afford to pay his usual fee. It wasn't unusual for one of his big clients to ask him to represent a company employee, for example, someone involved in a small civil suit or even a real estate matter. He handled those cases for just a few hundred dollars. Of course, a very good lawyer like Mr. Jerome rarely had any trouble winning such cases for the clients, and he was always glad to do it on his own time."

Festschrift looked over at me knowingly. His point had been proved. Another champion of the people. But he didn't know what I knew and that gave me a delicious, albeit guilty, feeling.

# SIX

Back in the car, Festschrift radioed in that we were back on the street:

"Oh-nine-six-H to central."

"Central, go ahead six-H."

"I'm ten-eight in the Loop."

And received word that he was to call his office:

"Ten-four, six-H. Oh, six-H?"

"Yeah."

"I've got a ten-twenty-one from your office here for you."

As soon as he was out of the worst of the traffic, Wally shot down a side street and headed for a pay phone. "Might be something good if they don't wanna tell me over the box."

While he was on the phone the dispatcher called for him again. "Oh-nine-six-H." I didn't know whether to answer for him or not. I waited.

"Central to oh-nine-six-H," came the call again.

I grabbed the mike. "Oh-nine-six-H is, uh, he's uh, he's on the phone."

"Ah, ten-four. Advise six-H to change that previous message to a ten-twenty-two."

"OK. I mean, ten-four."

He was mad when he returned to the car. "I told you to come in, not call in, Sergeant," he mimicked his lieutenant. "How am I supposed to know? The dispatcher says call, I call. It wasn't my fault the dispatcher got it wrong."

"The dispatcher called while you were on the phone and changed the message from a twenty-one to a twenty-two."

"Beautiful," he said, screeching away from the curb. "Now it's so hot the junior deputy in blue has to tell me in person and not even on the telephone. It better be good."

In the five minutes it took us to wend our way through the midafternoon rush to the Homicide Detail headquarters, Wally cooled down enough to resume his rundown of the victims and how he felt they tied together. "Victim number five is this TV producer gal, Frances Downs. And you know what she's known for?"

"You mean other than television?"

"No, I mean television."

"Yeah, I know she's in TV and known for that. Does good work and all that, has won a few awards, local and national."

"C'mon, Philip, specifics. What's her bag in television, and if you tell me producing or some other such obvious baloney I'm gonna open your door and take a hard left."

I got the feeling I was taking the heat he'd like to have given his lieutenant, a man more than ten years his junior. "Ah, you mean what kinda programs."

"You got it. What kinda programs is she known for?"

"I dunno."

Festschrift rolled his eyes and shrugged. "I bet you can *guess.*"

Programs spotlighting the down-and-outers?"

"Praise be. A shiny star for you. Frances Downs likes to produce shows that emphasize the plight and the accomplishments of the poor, ethnic, underprivileged in Chicago. She's—"

"Central to oh-nine-six-H, did you get that ten-twenty-two?" the radio interrupted. Angrily Wally grabbed the mike and depressed the button.

"Yes, sir, Mister Dispatcher. Mister zee-ro-ninety-six Homicide is just now ten-sixin' at Homicide HQ, ten-four?"

"Ten-four, six-H," the dispatcher said timidly. "Sorry, Wally."

"You'd better wait here," Wally said. "I shouldn't be long."

I trotted to a pay phone at the corner. "Hi, Bonnie, let me talk to Earl. . . . Hi, Earl, it's Philip. . . . Good. Listen, all Wally seems to have at this point are some interesting characteristics about each of the victims that might tie them together somewhat, things like the fact that all appear to have had a soft spot for the underprivileged. They were selfless types, and Wally is trying to make that fit with something he heard from a police-appointed psychologist who believes that the murderer is someone who is, in effect, killing himself over and over. Maybe someone who's nice but wishes he weren't."

"Is Wally convinced the perpetrator is male?"

"No, he doesn't know yet."

"And he's not onto Shannon yet?"

"Could be. He just got called into his headquarters. What do you want me to do if that's the news?"

"Hold off telling him for a while. If they think she's a prime suspect, they'll probably not want to scare her off. Let him discover that she's not working and not at home and then see what he wants to do. If he recommends an all-points bulletin, that will blow the secrecy and all the cops will know, and you know what that means."

"That the media will know too, and then the whole town."

"Right. And the more we talk to her here, the more convinced I am that she's not involved in the murders. She's a little weak on her memory of some of the murder dates, but I'm still banking on my judgment of character. I've been fooled before, but if this girl is a mass murderer, I'm the Easter Bunny."

"Here comes Wally. So what do you want me to do if he says anything about an all-points bulletin? Quick."

"Tell him we've got her, but swear him to secrecy first. Don't mess it up. It won't be easy but don't mess it up."

"Gotta go."

I tried to read Wally's walk as he headed for the car, tucking a document into his coat. When we were both in the car he put the key in the ignition but didn't start it up. "Bingo," he said softly, giving me a tight-lipped smile. "Persistence and modern technology pay off."

"Oh?" I said, trying not to betray nervousness.

"We've got a woman who's linked to three of the victims."

"Really? Who?"

"She lives on the same block as Ng, and if I'da been on the case that early, I'd have questioned her myself. I didn't talk to neighbors when we started the double-checking after the second murder. I just questioned his landlady and his boss."

I tried to steady my breathing.

"Anyway, her name came up on the client list of the dentist, McDough, which they just ran through the computer this morning. It was quite a list and get this, you know *why* it was quite a list?"

I wasn't listening. "Huh? No, why?"

"Because the guy has two offices. One within walking distance of his Marina City Tower condo and the other on the south side. Philip, it's a free clinic."

"Uh-huh."

"Uh-huh is all you can say? We've got a downtown dentist here who can afford a condo at Marina City, and he runs a charity clinic on the side. Does it fit? Has Wally put a team together?"

"Yeah, I guess."

"The problem is, Philip, that the lists don't often help. Here I've got a warrant for the arrest of a girl who lives in the neighborhood of the first victim and is a client of the last, and the mother of the second to last recognized the name when my boss called her. Mrs. Downs said, yes, this woman was an acquaintance, that she remembered the name and believes she was at the funeral. So what does my list mean? What do all these interesting characteristics mean? We don't know. Because we don't know anything about, um . . ." he dug the warrant out of his pocket, "Shannon Perry."

I said nothing.

He looked at his watch. "Still time to catch her at work," he said. "She's at some two-bit FM station in the Loop." And he started the car.

While he was busy driving, I mustered the breath to speak casually. "It sounds like a real break," I said. "But could it be coincidence?"

"Oh, highly unlikely. Three outa six ain't bad. I gotta admit I'd like something a little more solid on her relationship with each of these, but my boss has people on that right now. Living in the same block as a dead guy is no crime, and neither is happening to know someone in your profession. Goin' to the dentist seems like a crime, but in and of itself, it's not incriminating. Point is, a judge thinks three times is the charm and I hafta agree. Don't you?"

My mind was racing.

"Philip?"

"Yeah I guess. Sure."

"You thought it would be more exciting than this, did you? Sometimes this is all there is. You search and search and then a few things cross-match and all of a sudden you've got prime suspect number one. I wish I could say it was something I did, but if this is right and we get a killer off the streets, hey, what more can we ask for, huh?"

He grabbed the mike as an afterthought and informed central that oh-nine-six Homicide was ten-eight in the Loop. "You know how wet behind the ears my boss is?" he said gleefully, as if he could hardly contain himself now that he had a good suspect.

"No."

"My badge number is oh-nine-six, right? His has four digits!" And he roared.

I expected him to leap from the car when we cruised up to a small cubbyhole of an entrance that read *WMTR-FM, Metro Radio, Chicago* on its glass door. But he parked a few doors down and turned off the engine. "I wanna do this without scarin' anybody off or giving myself away as a cop. If she's not here, there's no sense everybody in there knowing that we're after her."

"You want me to ask for her? I can do it innocently enough."

"But can you get her to come with you?"

"Yeah, I'll tell her her car lights are on."

"How do you know her car is here? Where do they park?"

"I dunno."

"Forget it. What if she doesn't drive? Then she'll be suspicious and we'll lose her."

He turned the ignition switch far enough to keep the radio on. "Oh-nine-six-H is ten-six in the Loop."

"Ten-four."

"Sit tight, Philip.

A few minutes later Wally was back with the news that Miss Perry had taken a couple of weeks off. "That's not good news," he said, "but I didn't press for details because I didn't even want them to know why I was asking. The receptionist asked if I wanted to talk to her boss, but I said no. We've got her home address here."

He spread the warrant out in front of him. "It's way up on the north side, almost into Evanston. I think I'm gonna make one more stop before we go," he said. "Wanna try the radio?"

"Sure," I said, feeling more deceitful by the minute. I hoped Earl and Larry and Margo were taking advantage of every precious minute I was stalling for and were getting enough information to help clear Shannon.

"Tell the dispatcher that I'm back in the car and en route to South LaSalle Street where I'll be out of the car for a few minutes again. And do it all by the book."

"Where we going, Wally?"

"Where do you think? As long as we've got a minute, I want to see if we can find a link between this Perry woman and Dale Jerome."

My heart sank. "Oh-nine-six-H to central," I said.

"Central, go ahead."

"We're ten-eight and en route to South LaSalle where we'll be ten-six."

"Ten-four, six-H."

Wally clapped me on the shoulder in mock congratulation for a job well done on the radio, but I couldn't get enthusiastic. Lying by omission made me uncomfortable. Here I had hoped there'd be a lull in the investigation so I could raise some of the issues he and I had discussed during our last case. I wanted to know what he and Earl had talked about and what he thought of what Earl had to say. But Wally had been strangely silent about anything spiritual this time. It would have been natural for it to come up. The previous time, he had raised the question. And he had to know that Earl told us of their talks.

But then Wally was so immersed in this case, and now that it seemed to be breaking for him, it appeared there would be no time to talk of anything but leads and suspects. I knew that even when he discovered Shannon wasn't the prime suspect he thought she was, he would still consider it the biggest break of the case, because if she wasn't guilty, she had to be the reason someone was murdering these people.

As we parked near the law offices, Wally got a message to phone his office again. "Good grief, soldier blue is impatient today," he complained. "He wants to know what's happening every second. He's gonna want to know if I picked up the Perry girl and if so, why am I going somewhere else before I bring her in. Dumb."

In the lobby of the office building, Wally made his call. I could hear his condescending tone from a few feet away. "If I had picked up the girl, I'd be delivering her right now—sir. She's not at work, and she lives all the way up almost to Wisconsin. . . . No, I'm exaggerating. She's on the far north side, just south of Howard Street. But I wanna see if I can link her with Jerome before I make the trip. . . . Yes, I'll be making the trip anyway, but don't you think a fourth link would nail the lid on this coffin? . . . Yes, sir. . . . Yes, sir. I will."

He slammed the phone down. "He told me to get going

up north immediately." He stood thinking for a moment. "I can't. I just can't. Let's go."

He quickly shuffled to the elevator, and when we emerged he actually got ahead of me in the hall. "Miss Severinsen is gone," the receptionist said. "Home, I presume."

"Where is that?"

"Park Ridge."

"I haven't got time to go to Park Ridge. Can I see Jerome's files?"

"Well, I don't know, I—"

"I can get a warrant. Make this easy, huh?"

"Let me talk to Mr. Norris."

"No, let *me* talk to him. Get 'im out here."

When an irate-looking Mr. Norris emerged, Festschrift showed his badge and led him to a quiet corner. "I hate to cause you any trouble, sir, but I need access to Mr. Jerome's files right now. I'm sure you want the murderer caught as much as any of us do, and we have reason to believe it could have been one of his clients."

Without a word, Mr. Norris led Wally and me back to Jerome's empty office and unlocked six file cabinets. "Have at it," he said. "Need any help?"

"No, and thanks. We'll let you know when we leave."

"Philip, look up Perry, and I'll check under the call letters of the radio station."

I raced quickly through and found nothing, then stepped quickly over to the file for Field Enterprises, owners of the *Sun-Times* and the now defunct *Daily News*. Wally was just slamming his file drawer shut when I found the name, "Perry, S., auto, civil suit, see auxiliary file." He was walking over.

I straightened up and shut the drawer. "Nothing," I said, feeling rotten.

"Shoot," he said in a hiss, jamming his hands into his pockets. He paced the room for a few seconds, then headed toward Mr. Norris's door. He knocked and entered and I followed. It was obvious we had interrupted a client consultation. "I'm sorry," Wally said.

"No problem," Norris said. "Excuse me just a moment." He stepped outside. "Find what you need?"

"No. Would Jerome have had any other files, like on cases he did on his own time and not for your firm?"

"His secretary would have taken those. She's the executor of his will."

"I need to see those. Would you be able to release her phone number?"

"Certainly."

He led Wally and me back out to the receptionist, where he instructed her to find Miss Severinsen's number. She pursed her lips and hesitated, whereupon Mr. Norris quietly said, "Right now."

"And may I use your phone?" Wally asked her. Her anger was obvious.

"Yes, you may," Norris said firmly. "Why don't you take a little break, Margaret." Angrily she walked away. "Just dial nine, Sergeant," Norris said.

Festschrift explained his urgent need to Miss Severinsen and asked her to check the files for Shannon Perry and to call his dispatcher with a message of simply either positive or negative and it would be relayed to him. "Thanks a million. I'll let you know how this turns out, and please don't mention anything about this to anyone."

Sergeant Walvoord F. Festschrift was psyched. I could have enjoyed it, and him, if I didn't feel so lousy about leading him on this wild-goose chase. He was gathering information he would eventually need, but I could have saved him all the effort. We weren't far north of the Loop when the dispatcher radioed that Wally's lieutenant had been trying to get hold of him and that he was to call in as soon as possible. Wally jumped on the mike. "Tell Lieutenant Merrill oh-nine-six is en route to the north side and that if he needs to talk to me about anything else, I'm here."

Apparently that was all the pesky lieutenant had wanted. We were near the Hollywood exit off Lake Shore Drive when another message came over the radio. "Central to oh-nine-six-H."

"Go ahead, central."

"You were expecting a message from a Miss Severinsen?"

"Ten-four."

"Message follows: positive."

Wally looked over at me and extended his fat hand for a slap. I gave him five and wished I could die.

# SEVEN

When Wally made his first pass of Shannon's two-story apartment building—hers was the upstairs flat—he asked me to jot down the license number of the car parked at the curb. Then he pulled around the corner out of sight of her building and shifted into park.

"Oh-nine-six-H to central," he said.

"Central, go."

"I need a ten-twenty-eight on Illinois plate JE-nine-nine-two-eight."

"Stand by, six-H."

I was in no mood to talk as we waited. Wally didn't want conversation either, but he did talk to himself. "Four out of six, whew! Wonder how she hooks up with Matacena and Pritkin. She wouldn't have wasted her own pastor, though she *did* blow away her dentist. Hmph. You wouldn't put a woman together with this M.O., would you?"

He wasn't asking me, so I didn't answer.

"Maybe she's a big girl," he said. He looked at his watch and then around the neighborhood. "Nobody at the windows as far as I can tell." He sniffed. The man was a terrible waiter. So was I. I jumped when the radio crackled.

"Central to six-H."

"Yeah, gimme it."

"Your ten-twenty-eight on JE-nine-nine-two-eight. Registered to a blue/grey 'eighty-one Ford Granada two-door hardtop. Owner Perry, Shannon, no middle name, born nine-nine-'fifty-six, female, white, seventy-five-fifty-five North Hoyne Street, Chicago six-oh-six-four-five. Five-foot-five, one hundred fifteen pounds, brown hair, blue eyes, no restrictions, no violations, not reported stolen."

Wally thanked the dispatcher and told me to be ready to run around to the back entrance, "in case she meets us as we come up the walk and decides to make a run." I nodded, knowing we were opening an empty package.

As we left the car he pointed down an alley that led to the rear. We buzzed her from the first floor. When he got no response, he said, "You'd better scoot around back," but before I could, the landlord poked his head out of his first-floor flat. "Can you let me upstairs fast?" Wally said, producing his badge.

"She ain't up there," the man said. "Hasn't been around since Sunday night when she stopped in to get her things and then left with a scruffy lookin' young guy in a little yellow car."

"You know him?"

"Nope. Never saw him before. Looked like a construction worker or somethin'. Dressed that way anyway. None too big. You don't got trouble with her, do ya, Captain? My guess is yer after the guy. He's a drifter, ain't he?"

"Yeah, something like that. Listen, you hear from her or see either one of 'em, you call me at this number, huh?"

"Right, Captain."

Wally looked dejected trudging back to the car. He

swore. "Somethin's goin' down," he said. "At least my boss can't tell me I would have had her if I hadn't taken the time to visit Jerome's office. I'm not looking forward to this call."

"This call?"

"I gotta tell Merrill that she's blown."

He went around to his side of the car, and I asked him over the top, "What happens then?"

"He puts out an APB and she becomes an instant fugitive. She'll be much harder to find this way, I can tell you that."

"I can't let you do that," I said as he opened his door. He had started to climb in the car, but now he straightened up, his hand on the open door. "You can't let me do what?"

"Have them put out an APB on Shannon Perry."

His face screwed itself into the most puzzled expression he could muster and he cocked his head. With half a laugh he managed, "Wha . . . ?"

"I know where she is," I said, wondering if he was going to go for his gun and drop me.

He was speechless. He squinted at me. "I've never thought much of your sense of humor, Spence," he said. "But you had better not be serious."

"I'm serious, Wally. I know where Shannon Perry is."

His wheels were turning. "Does Earl have her?"

"Yes, sir."

Wally took one step back and slammed his door so hard that it bounced back open and hit him. He kicked it shut on the rebound and something metallic broke loose. He spun in a circle and brought both fists crashing down on top of the car. I stood there, letting his eyes burn through me, hoping his anger would somehow vindicate me.

"I'm sorry I deceived you, Wally."

He couldn't talk. He just shook his head and stalked off down the sidewalk, once turning back as if to say something but deciding not to. He cursed in a loud, raspy whisper, and as he stomped along, his trench coat flailed in the breeze behind him. I moved to follow him.

"Get away from me!" he yelled over his shoulder.

"Hadn't you better call in?" I said.

"Get away!"

"Wally, they're going to send help here if they don't hear from you, aren't they?"

"And what am I supposed to call in?" he demanded, stopping and turning around, hands on his hips.

I looked down.

He came back, closing the gap between us and shoving his red, sweating face next to mine. The veins in his forehead and neck werc bulging. He whispered, "Huh? What am I supposed to call in?" He swore again. "Am I supposed to tell them that my partner, my unofficial in . . . uh, in . . . intern or whatever you call yourself and my old friend from the division have been harboring the prime suspect in a mass murder case?"

He was about to explode. I didn't know what to say. Telling him I thought we could prove she was as innocent a victim as the deceased would have only set him off more. He had my lapel in his fist.

"Let me explain," I said.

"Oh, you'll explain all right," he snarled. "But let me tell you something first. I don't much care how this shakes down, but I wanna impress on your brain what it means to give your life for something. We're talking about total devotion here, Spence. Oh, yeah, I've told you about the fun of this job, but you've also seen some of the drudgery. And you've only seen the tip of the iceberg. Do you have any idea how many personal, one-on-one interviews I've conducted since Friday, September 3, when Annamarie Matacena was found with her brains blown out? Of course you don't. Nobody does.

"And can you imagine how I felt September 6 and September 22 and October 16 and then last Thursday? I'm out here from the time I get up in the morning until the time I crash into the sack around midnight every night, seven '  days a week, and I don't sleep too good because with all the work I been doin', I'm not gettin' any closer to the murderer. I can feel it when I get closer, and I haven't been. Until now, all I had was a list of nice-guy victims and a psychologist tellin' me it's really a suicide. Well, lead me to the suicidal murderer so I can help her finish the job.

"I don't know how this Perry woman fell into your laps, but you can bet it wasn't because you been poundin' the streets for two months!" Festschrift released his grip, took two long strides to my side of the car, and kicked a huge dent in the door. "Today was a typical day, Spence," he said, still shaking his head. "Interviews in the morning, then a seminar with the psychologist, a fast lunch, then downtown, back to see the boss, over to the radio station, back to the lawyer's office, then up here. This is what it's like. You see why I dream about breaks like these? Do you?"

I nodded, but it didn't slow him down.

"You let me go to that radio station and all the way up here? You probably knew there was a connection with Jerome, too."

I nodded dejectedly, almost feeling as if I should admit that I saw her name in Jerome's files at the downtown office. I resisted the urge.

Festschrift was puffing and sweating and I feared for his health. He went around to the driver's side and opened the back door. He shed both coats and flung them in the back-seat, slammed the door, wrenched the front open, and slid behind the wheel. He had started the car and shifted into drive before I realized I was still standing outside the car. I jumped in as he pulled away, but I found it difficult to even look at him.

"Central to oh-nine-six-H, come in, please," came the urgent sound of the dispatcher.

"Yeah, I'm here."

"You need assistance, six-H?"

"Negative."

"Your office requests immediate status report."

"I'll ten-twenty-one 'im, ten-four?"

"Negative, six-H. Lieutenant Merrill is right here."

A new voice came on. "Festschrift, what do you think you're doing up there? Have you got the subject or not? You need help? What's the story?"

"Negative. Suspect has been located. Can you meet me in Glencoe?"

"Glencoe?"

I put my hand on Festschrift's arm. "You can't bring your boss to see her," I whispered.

"Stand by, sir," Festschrift said. "I'll be right back to you."

He slammed on the brakes, sending us both into the dash. Throwing the mike on the floor, making the spring cord bounce and dangle, he pushed his meaty index finger near my nose. "Listen, Philip, that's enough. I'm gonna do anything I please and if you or your boss or anybody up there interferes with the apprehension of this suspect, I'll bust every one of you for harboring a class-X felony sus-pect and obstructing justice. You got that?"

He was trembling. So was I. I nodded. "Can you at least ask him to come alone?"

"I don't care if he brings the national guard."

"Festschrift, get back on the blower!" Merrill was shouting.

"I'm back," Wally said. "Let me give you an address where you can meet me and have access to the subject."

"You're sure the subject will be there?"

Wally looked at me. I nodded. "Affirmative. One more thing, sir. Come alone."

"Come again?"

"Come alone."

There was a pause, then a resigned voice. "Ten-four, Wally. This had better be good."

We were about twenty minutes from Earl's office, and Wally knew it would take Lieutenant Merrill another forty-five minutes from the Loop at this time of day, so he pulled off the road. "I don't want to get there before Merrill does. I'm not sure what I'd say to Earl."

"You know Earl's got an explanation."

"Oh, sure, and I can't wait to hear it."

"Can I call him?"

"Not on your life."

It was still hard to face Wally. He looked out his window and I looked out mine. Darkness was falling fast as we sat and listened to the static traffic on the Motorola. With nothing to say I was able to concentrate for the first time on the stench in that car. *Years and years worth of drunks and cigarette butts,* I thought, *not to mention your basic grime.* Then it hit me. "Hey Wally, you've quit smoking!"

He turned slowly to get a full look at the idiot who would think of something like that at a time like this. "Yes," he said patronizingly, "I did."

"Well, that's good. I think that's good. Don't you think that's good?"

"Yes, it's good."

"I mean, you feel better, don't you?"

"Yes, I feel better. Thank you."

"Well, good. You're welcome. I mean, good." I slapped my knees and looked out the window into the night.

"Hey, Wally?"

After a pause, "Yes?"

"You're not mad, are you?"

His laugh started deep in his belly and shook him from head to toe. It came out first as a low wheeze and grew to a great roar, culminating in a series of shrill, falsetto hoots I thought would wake the dead. He buried his face in his hands and continued to bounce long after the sound had died away. As my remark continued to work on him he would laugh anew, muffling it in his palms. He laughed until he cried and the tears poured through his fingers, and I wasn't sure he was crying from laughing or crying because of the emotional investment he had spent on me, getting off his chest the frustration of this most taxing task.

For the next several minutes, as he wiped the tears away, little bursts of laughter would squeak out against his will, and he would shake his head and look at me and laugh some more.

"You're gonna drain me of all the wrath I was saving for Earl," he managed.

"You *saved* some?" I said, and he burst into laughter again.

After a while he looked at his watch and slowly pulled away. "We'll have the residents calling the cops on us soon," he said.

"Can I tell you what we're doing with your prime suspect at our place?" I said.

"Yeah. Give me a head start. Why should I have any more surprises today?"

I told him that Shannon had approached Larry before

she had become a suspect and that Earl and Larry had invited her to stay in our custody during her two weeks off.

"Larry is convinced she's got alibis. Earl is getting more confident."

"Larry's the owner of that canary yellow car, isn't he?"

"Uh-huh."

"So he was the construction-worker type who spirited Shannon Perry away Sunday night. How is Larry?"

"He was OK until now. He's pretty worried about Shannon."

"He oughta be, Philip. She's in big, bad trouble."

"But she turned herself in."

"To the wrong people. And you can't really call looking for help turning yourself in. She's scared to death, and she's looking for 'any port,' as they say."

"The point is, Wally, if she does have alibis, there's no way around the fact that whoever's committing the murders is doing it for its effect on her."

"For sure. But forgive me if it takes me a while to move too quickly away from her as a suspect and to her as a victim. I mean, I've got a girl here who's linked with four of six murder victims, remember."

"Six."

"Six?"

"She's connected with all six."

"How is she connected with Matacena?"

"She ran into her at the hospital when she was doing a story on pediatrics."

"And Pritkin?"

"She only attended a wedding he officiated."

"That would have taken awhile to put together. All six, huh?" Festschrift let out a long whistle through his teeth. "You know we're going to have to take this girl into custody until we can verify her alibis, don't you?"

"I suppose."

"We won't be able to verify them on a Monday night, you know. At least I don't see how we can."

"But if she's a target, rather than the murderer, can't you use her to catch him?"

"It's possible."

"But if there's any publicity about your taking a suspect into custody, won't that blow that angle?"

"There doesn't have to be any noise. My boss is a reasonable man. Grief, I can't believe I just said that. But seriously, for whatever faults he has, he knows the difference between a victim and a perpetrator, and the sooner we can determine which Shannon Perry is, the better shot we'll have at the murderer."

"How were you able to get a warrant for someone's arrest for murder who was not seen with the victims on the days they were murdered?"

"For one thing, we don't know she wasn't seen with them. The lieutenant will be able to tell us more on that. But in a case like this, it's not at all hard to get a warrant to pick someone up on suspicion of murder when their name is linked to two, let alone three of the deceased. It grew to four by midday and now you tell me she's at least remotely connected to all six. Put yourself in a judge's position, even ignoring the public and media hysterics after going this long without a lead. Would you issue a warrant for Shannon Perry's arrest?"

I pretended to think for a moment. There was only one answer of course. "Sure."

Wally waited at the corner near our building for the sight of a blue-and-white carrying Lieutenant Merrill. When it appeared, two men were in the front seat. It followed us into the parking lot of the EH office, and Wally rolled down his window facing the other car's passenger side. "You couldn't come alone?" he asked. "Be cool. He's leaving. You're going to drive me and the suspect back downtown. Now tell me what's going on and who's that?"

When Wally had finished briefing him, Merrill stepped out. He was a youngish forty, prematurely gray, and trim. He looked none too pleased that all the lights were off on the second floor. Neither did Wally.

# EIGHT

The office was closed and locked. No one was in Earl's or my rooms, and I wasn't sure I wanted to tell Lieutenant Merrill or Sergeant Festschrift that they could all be in the apartment at the end of the hall.

"I don't guess they'd venture out in public for dinner," I said.

Merrill gave me a look I thought had been patented by Wally.

"They must be at Bonnie's," I said. "Should I call over there?"

"Sure, and scare 'em off?" Wally said. "Forget it. Just take us there."

On the way, Lieutenant Merrill sat stonily in the backseat. "So, what do you think Sergeant?" he said finally. "Is the woman armed and dangerous and should we approach it that way, or do we step in nice and cordial-like and depend on the level-headedness of the former head of Chicago Homicide. That is the Earl Haymeyer we're talking about, isn't it?"

"One and the same."

"He's an impressive fellow."

"You know him?" Wally and I said in unison.

"Only by reputation. Remember he was a few bosses before me, but he's the one who left the longest-lasting mark on the operation. His systems and procedures and standards are pretty much still intact, and anybody who was around back then has nothing but praise for him."

"Except me," Festschrift said.

"Right, except you. Except I don't believe a word you say. Did you give Haymeyer as bad a time as you give me?"

"Worse."

"I'd have to see that to believe it. I can tell deep down you liked Haymeyer. You'd have had to unless you were a real bozo. And much as I'd like to, I can't lay that rap on you."

"I guess that was a compliment," Festschrift said.

"Yeah, and the way you treat me must be your form of compliment, especially if you treated Haymeyer the same way."

"I didn't. I said it was worse."

"Then you must have liked him more."

"Of course."

I couldn't believe the good mood. Apparently these men had enough confidence in Earl that they felt there was little danger either that Shannon Perry was the murderer or that they'd lose her if she was.

"We doin' this by the book or not, boss?" Wally said as we pulled into the parking lot at Bonnie's apartment.

"How do you mean?"

"Code says we have guns drawn on a felony arrest, and we go in loud, badges out."

"Forget it. We're just making a social call on Mr. Haymeyer and his friends. If one of his friends happens to be Shannon Perry, we have a little piece of mail for her."

"You're the boss."

"Thanks for reminding me. Remind yourself occasionally."

I rang the bell at Bonnie's door and heard the conversation cease inside. Someone stepped to the door and, I assume, was looking through the peep hole. I waved self-consciously. "It's Philip and Sergeant Festschrift and someone else!" Bonnie said, opening the door. We heard Earl call out, "Wait!" but it was too late. Festschrift stepped past me and through the door before Bonnie could even think to shut it again.

The three of us moved past Bonnie, who was wearing a large apron to cover her clothes, and we were met by a dinner table surrounded by people who had just started eating. Margo and Larry and Earl and Shannon Perry stared at us over steaming plates. "Ah, real good work, Philip," Earl said, and I tried to laugh but nothing came out.

"Well, let me get some more chairs and you men can join us. How'll that be?" Bonnie said.

"I don't think . . ." Wally started to say.

"Nonsense, Sergeant," Merrill said. "I haven't eaten dinner. Have you?"

"Well, no."

"Then we'd be delighted. Thank you, ma'am."

Bonnie and Larry searched for more chairs while Margo rummaged for more plates. Everybody scooted around, and soon eight of us were shoulder to shoulder around Bonnie's dining room table.

There was an awkward silence, everyone ignoring the obvious, until Merrill spoke. "You must be Earl Haymeyer," he said, shaking hands.

"And you must be the current head of Homicide."

"You say current as if you consider the job transitory."

"It has been. I'm sure you'll spring from it to bigger and better things."

"As you did?"

"Well I wouldn't say that. I . . ."

"Oh, of course you did. And did this rascal give you as much trouble then as he does me now?"

"Well, I used to work for him, you know. I guess I gave him a little trouble myself before the tables were turned. I imagine I deserved whatever he dished out."

"Well, I don't deserve it!"

And there we all sat, most of us laughing, some of us staring, and one young, dark-haired girl focusing wide-eyed on the head of Chicago Homicide and unable to bring her fork to her mouth.

"Dessert now or later?" Bonnie asked as she began to clear the table.

"This isn't my party," Lieutenant Merrill said, "but it's about to be. Ma'am, you invited me in here and you can throw me out, but Sergeant Festschrift and I would like permission to talk to Mr. Haymeyer and Mr. Spence and Miss Perry in another room, if we may."

"Certainly," Bonnie said, and she ushered us into her living room, where Earl and Shannon sat on the couch and Merrill and I sat on the coffee table. Wally sat on the arm of the couch.

"Miss Perry," the lieutenant began, "you and I have some serious talking to do."

"I understand," she said softly.

"I'm afraid I have to tell you that you are under arrest on suspicion of murder in the first degree. You have the right to remain silent. Anything you say can and will be held against you in a court of law. You have the right to have an attorney present while you are being questioned. If you cannot afford one, an attorney will be appointed for you. Do you understand these rights as I have read them to you?"

"Yes," she said, barely audibly.

"And do you wish to have an attorney present?"

"No."

"Do I understand you correctly that you are waiving your right to an attorney for the purpose of this questioning?"

"Yes."

"And will you also waive the right to silence?"

"Yes."

"Good. Is there anyone here you would rather not have present?"

"No."

"And is there anyone you would like present who is not here?"

"Yes, could Larry be with me?"

"Certainly."

Larry joined us and squeezed onto the couch between Earl and Shannon.

"Are you armed?" Merrill asked Shannon.

"No."

"Do you own a weapon?"

"You mean of any kind?"

' Yes."

"I have one of those Mace cannisters, and I carry a sharp instrument on my key ring."

"Do you own a gun?"

"No."

"Have you ever owned a gun of any type?"

"No."

"Do you know of anyone who owns a handgun?"

"I think Larry does."

Larry nodded.

"Have you ever handled Mr. Shipman's handgun?"

"No, I've never seen it."

"Did you know Lawson Ng of Hoyne Avenue in Chicago?"

"I didn't really know him. I knew who he was, spoke to him occasionally. I don't think he knew my name."

"Did he ever help you change a tire on your car?"

Shannon looked surprised. "Why yes, I had forgotten about that."

"Do you remember when that was?"

"No. Well . . . I know it was hot out."

"So it was during the summer?"

"I think so. It was very hot."

"Could it have been June first?"

"Yes, it could have been. I remember it was his day off. He was jogging or something and noticed I had a flat."

"Are you aware that he was murdered that day?"

"No, I thought it was the next day."

"His body was discovered the next day, but the coroner puts the time of death as late afternoon, June 1, a Wednesday."

"I was at work at that time."

"Can that be proven?"

"Oh yes, there are careful records."

"But you don't punch a clock, do you, Miss Perry?"

"No, but our office coordinator keeps a careful record of how much time we spend on our various projects for purposes of cost control. I'm certain she would have a record that shows I was in the office from late morning—I was late because of the tire—until early evening."

"Did you mention the help Mr. Ng gave you to anyone in the office?"

Shannon thought a moment. "Yes, I think I told Chuck Childers, our morning man. I was going with him at the time, or we had just broken up, I don't remember. Anyway, we have always been on good terms and I'm sure I mentioned it to him."

"And was it an item in your office when the Ng murder was announced?"

"Well, yes. Everyone wanted to know if I knew him and how close I lived to him and all that. In all the excitement I must have forgotten about the tire-changing thing until now."

"Tell me about your relationship with Frances Downs."

"I didn't know her well. I always respected her and felt that she did good work. Mostly I was impressed with how she concentrated much of her work on the underprivileged."

I stole a glance at Wally, who was scribbling notes. He broke in with a question. "Did you mention that to anyone?"

"You mean about respecting her for that?"

"Right."

"Oh, yes, I suppose that's all I ever said about Frances. I'm sure people got tired of hearing me say that."

"Somebody apparently did," Wally said.

Merrill took over again. "Were you aware that Miss Downs was what some would call a 'kept woman'?"

"You mean that someone was paying for that big apartment at Sandburg?"

"You're aware of that then?"

"Of the apartment, yes. Everyone knew about it."

"Did anyone wonder how she could afford it?"

"I guess we all figured she had a guy. No one knew who, though. It could have been any one of a number of men. I tried not to talk about her in those terms. I'm not a goody-goody or anything like that, but I usually talked only about the positive things about Frances, because there were many. I didn't figure it was any of my business if she was whatever you say she was."

"Who's your dentist?"

"Dr. McDough."

"Dr. Thomas McDough in the Loop?"

"Yes."

"When did you see him last?"

"In October, I believe."

"October 29, a Friday?"

"That's possible. Yes, it could have been. I don't remember exactly."

"You didn't see him after that—socially, on the street, anywhere for any reason?"

"Not that I recall."

"He wasn't in your offices during the first week of this month?"

"Yes! I'm sorry. He was. I don't know what he came in for, but he was in to see somebody and he ducked in and waved at me. I didn't even speak to him."

Merrill looked concerned, as if he didn't like these sudden recalls of memory. "And did you say anything about him to anyone?"

"I may have said something to either Chuck or Jake Raven, our boss. I don't think I said he was my dentist, but I said we ought to do a story on his free clinic on the south side sometime."

"And when he was murdered did you mention that he was your dentist?"

"No, by that time I was getting paranoid because I had been acquainted with so many of these victims. I didn't say anything about it at all."

"You didn't mention to the girls in the office that the dead man was the one who had come through the week before?"

"No."

"And you didn't say anything about it to the one you suggested the special program to?"

"No."

"And whoever that was said nothing to you about McDough?"

"No."

"Are you aware how implausible that sounds?"

"I guess. But it's the truth."

Merrill stood to stretch, leaned down and whispered to Festschrift. "Did you say she's linked to the others as well?"

"There's evidence of that, yeah."

"You wanna ask a few questions?"

"Sure."

Merrill sat back down. "Miss Perry, do you mind answering some more questions?"

"Not at all, especially if it'll keep me from having to go downtown and being booked or whatever."

"I can't guarantee that it will," the lieutenant said. "We cannot, of course, take only your word for these alibis, you know."

"But they should be easy enough to check," Larry said.

"By whom? Would you like to start verifying them tonight?"

"I would."

"Well, you probably would, but I can't let you do that. Let's continue here, and I'll have to decide what we're going to do with Miss Perry in light of this warrant. Sergeant Festschrift?"

"Yeah, Shannon, you don't mind if I call you by your first name, do you?"

"No."

"Isn't it also true that you are at least somewhat acquainted with the second, third, and fourth victims in this murder spree?"

"Yes, I'm afraid so. That's why I asked Larry for help. It was beginning to frighten me."

"I can see how it would. Now, as I understand it, you had only one contact with Annamarie Matacena?"

"Yes, she was sort of my guide when I was researching a story at the hospital where she works."

"Did you know where she lived or anything else about her?"

"No. Nothing. In fact, I only remembered her name from her nameplate and then from the name of the hospital when her murder was reported."

"And of course you made mention of it at the office."

"Yes, several of us had been at the hospital."

"Who, specifically?"

"Well, Jeanie, another writer; Steve Lacey, our part-time sound man; and Jake."

"Your boss was there?"

"Yes. He's teaching Steve how to do sound engineering, so he went along on that trip to show Steve what to do when the actual interview crew went back."

"And who would have been on that crew?"

"An announcer. I'm not sure which one, maybe Chuck. Then a sound man, probably Steve. And one assistant, either me or Jeanie."

"Well, did you go back or not?"

"I don't think we ever did. That job may still be in the hopper."

"Why hasn't it been done yet?"

"I really don't know. I thought Chuck was going to be the announcer on it and so I told him what to look for, but I never heard if the show was done, and I probably would have heard if it had. Maybe the murder of the woman who worked there made it seem inappropriate for now."

"Is there anything you want to tell me about the Reverend Mr. Pritkin, other than that you attended a wedding at his church when he officiated?"

"No, I think that's all. I think everyone from work was there."

"By everybody you mean . . . ?"

"Our office coordinator, Jeanie, Jake took me, Steve wasn't there, and I guess neither was Chuck. Somebody from the night crew came."

"Whose wedding was it?"

"A girl who used to do the traffic for us on 'afternoon drivetime.' "

"Did Reverend Pritkin make any impression on you?"

"No, not really."

"Did you know he was an unusual man at all?"

"Unusual? In what way?"

"I'm asking you."

"Well, yes, now that you mention it. The girl, wow, I don't even remember her name now, but the bride told us that when the pastor heard they were both putting themselves through college, he refused to accept a fee and wouldn't even accept any money for the use of the church."

"So that made an impression on you?"

"Yes."

"Would you have told anyone about that?"

"I might have."

"Would you have discussed it with anyone?"

"I might have discussed it with the people I went to the wedding with. We went out together afterward, even though I was sort of with Jake. We all went to dinner as I recall."

"And that was a topic of conversation? The fact that the pastor was really nice to the wedding couple?"

"Probably so."

"Would anyone at work have known that you were once represented by Dale Jerome in a civil suit?"

"Oh probably, though they might not have put the name with it."

"Why not?"

"I'm not sure I always used his name when I mentioned his kindness."

"But you might have talked to someone at work about it?"

"Sure."

"That's a big thing with you, isn't it?"

"What's that?"

"Talking about people who do things for you or for others?"

"Yes, I guess it is. I don't know enough people who go out of their way for others. I don't do it much myself."

"So, you talk about it?"

"I guess I do."

"You told people about Mr. Ng helping you with your tire. And you told them how nice Mrs. Matacena was. And it impressed you what a kind gesture Reverend Pritkin made to the young couple, even though you can't remember the bride's name. You remember a kindness from a high-paid lawyer from six years ago. You are so impressed with the soft spot in Frances Downs's heart for the underprivileged that you forgive her for her loose morals."

"I never thought of it that way."

"And your dentist, a part of life most people would rather not think or talk about, gets your vote of confidence because he runs a free clinic. You're almost too good to be true."

"I am? I don't think so. I don't think it's unique to be impressed by selfless people."

"Are you a selfless person?"

"No. I wish I were. Sometimes I am, but never enough. I'd really like to be."

"Why? Because they get nice things said about them or even their faults covered because of it?"

"No, it is just the way I was raised and I'd like to be that way."

"But you're not?"

"Not as much as I'd like to be."

"You were raised to be selfless?"

"Not exactly. But to be nice, do things for people. And if you can't say something nice about someone, don't say anything at all."

"How does that fit in with your profession? Newswriting is hardly ever good news."

"Maybe that's why I talk about people who do good things. I don't know. When I get a chance to do an in-depth piece, I usually go for something like that. There's enough bad news."

"How much does it bother you that you're not as good and selfless as you want to be?"

"I don't think I dwell on it. I hope it just encourages me to do better, to do more. I don't let it get to me."

"It doesn't get to you to the point where sometimes you feel you'd like to kill someone who's better than you are? Do you sometimes feel you'd like to murder them? Shoot them? In the head? In the brain? To get rid of that part of them that thinks such good thoughts that it allows them to be the nice, selfless person you just seem to be?"

We were all stunned at this performance by Festschrift. Even Earl was taken back. Merrill stared intently at Shannon. Margo and Bonnie had entered the room without our even noticing.

Shannon stared right back at Wally, but she didn't respond.

# NINE

Finally, Earl stood. "Is that the end of your questioning, Wally?" he said.

"Now just a minute," Lieutenant Merrill said, raising a hand. "I'm a guest here, but I *am* in charge of the questioning, and Miss Perry has not answered the question."

Shannon was trembling. "May I ask a question before I answer that one?" she said.

"Certainly," Festschrift said.

"I want to know if that's what you think."

"If what's what I think, honey?"

"If you think I murdered all those people because they were nice and I'm not."

"That's not for me to decide."

"You can sit there and accuse me of that and then tell me it's not for you to decide?"

"I didn't accuse you of anything, dear. I merely asked you a question."

"Please stop with your endearing names, and please don't call that diatribe you just finished a mere question. Did you ask me that because you think it's the case?"

"I asked you that for two reasons. I wanted to see if you would deny it, which you did not—"

"Well, I'll deny it—"

"Excuse me, Miss Perry. Which you *did not*. And I also asked it to see what kind of reaction I would get if you did *not* deny it."

"I'm denying it. No, I didn't kill anyone. I never even thought of it. And just because I admit I'm not always as selfless as I'd like to be is no reason to think I would kill anyone who is. I admire them. I talk about them. I don't go around murdering them. Can't a person admit a shortcoming without you thinking they're a murderer? Saying that I'm not always as selfless as I want to be is a bit of a selfless statement in itself."

Larry put his hand on Shannon's shoulder and shushed her.

"Let her talk," Wally insisted. "I want her to tell me that she's not all bad. That she does do some good things."

"Of course I do!" She was crying now. "I wasn't admitting to anything terrible. I told my boyfriend, or my former boyfriend, to look up Mrs. Matacena because she was so nice. I was complimenting her and making his job easier. Is there something wrong with that? What did you want me to say? That I'm perfect? That I always do things for others at my own expense? That I'm as nice as Mr. Jerome or Dr. McDough?"

She dropped her head and cried. "How did I get into this mess?" she sobbed. "I was just trying to answer truthfully, and he turned it all around."

Even Festschrift appeared a bit self-conscious, as if he felt he should defend what he had done to everyone glaring at him now. "She'll get tougher questions than that in court," he said.

Earl stood again. "Are we through now?"

Merrill looked to Festschrift who nodded. "I'm afraid we are going to have to take you downtown until we can check on your whereabouts at the time of each of these murders," Merrill said.

"Are you telling me that I'm going to be spending the night in jail?"

"It won't be that bad. We can keep you at the precinct lockup by yourself."

"And you don't think that'll be bad? Oh, Larry, do something!"

"Earl," Larry said, "can they take her downtown without a female officer in the car?"

"No, they can't," Earl said.

"That's right," Merrill said, "and that's why I was going to ask for the loan of either your secretary or Margo Franklin here."

"I'll go,"- Margo said.

"No, wait a minute," Earl said. "You're still working for me, right, Margo?"

"Of course."

"Then I'm telling you I don't want you to go. Lieutenant, you'll just have to have a matron come out here tonight. Otherwise you can leave her in my custody."

"Oh, come on, Haymeyer, be reasonable. You know how difficult it'll be to get a policewoman driven out here at this time of the night."

"You bet I do."

"What's the point of leaving her in your custody?"

"Several points. First, I believe every word she's said. Every one. Even the sudden memories. If she was lying she wouldn't try something that stupid. Second, I think her alibis are going to hold up, and there's no sense putting an innocent young woman in a jail cell. Third, I want to hear more about everyone in her office because, if I'm right and she's innocent, she's more than innocent, she's a catalyst. Someone is murdering these people because of her, and we'd better find out why. You take her downtown and it leaks out that you've got her. Whoever it is at that station who's committing these crimes will wrap himself into a cocoon you'll never penetrate."

Merrill appeared to be softening. "Earl, you realize the risk I'd be taking. This is the biggest murder case in Chicago since John Wayne Gacy. I'd be hung out to dry if something happened to my only suspect."

"I'll sign anything you want. You put her in my custody and I'll see that she stays put. She'll be here when you need her. Frankly, I think we're going to need her for bait eventually. It's up to you, Lieutenant. Either you trust me and leave her with me, or you can call downtown for a matron."

Merrill and Festschrift huddled alone for a moment. "All right, Earl," Merrill said finally. "I'm gonna trust you."

Shannon hugged Larry in relief.

"I hate to be so ornery about this, gentlemen," Earl said, seeing the men to the door. "But you were pretty tough on her, Wally."

"Forget it."

"Hey," I said, "can you take me downtown to my car?"

Festschrift motioned that I should follow him, and I almost forgot to kiss Margo good-bye. "I've missed you today," she said.

"Me too," I said. "I can't wait to tell you about it. You gonna be up when I get back?"

"Depends. Are you going to be talking with Festschrift until all hours like you did last time?"

"Hm. Probably so. Don't wait up for me. I'll talk to you when this thing's over."

"Who knows when that's going to be?"

Wally's car was idling by the time I raced into the parking lot and jumped in. The ride back to Chicago was pretty quiet. I got the impression that the two men had already discussed whether they had done the right thing, Wally in pushing as hard as he had and Merrill in leaving the suspect in Earl Haymeyer's custody.

Wally dropped his boss off at Homicide and then tooled over to the precinct house and pulled in beside my car. He turned his engine off and rolled his window half-way down. I was glad he appeared in a talking mood. "So, what'd ya learn your first day as an intern, huh?"

"Not to get you riled."

Wally appeared to laugh, but no sound came out. "Yeah, well, I'm not takin' back a word of it. Even now that I see the whole picture, I don't think Earl should have put you up to stalling me like that. Aside from all the grief it put me through, it's an insult to me. Look how it turned out; the girl is still with Earl and his people. We're not goons. Earl doesn't have to worry about us. We're reasonable people."

"I'm impressed."

"Don't be smart."

"I'm not. I'm serious."

Wally turned sideways toward me and rested his knee on the seat between us, wedging his foot into the Motorola. "Good to have that thing off for a while," he said.

"Oh, I still kinda think the radios are neat, listening to all that stuff."

"Aah, you get to the point where you tune out everything except your own numbers unless you hear certain codes, like B & E or something."

"Breaking and entering?"

"Right."

The fat man let out a long breath. "Whew, big day," he said. "Big, big day. I'm gonna sleep tonight, I'll tell you that."

"What time'll you get up tomorrow?"

"I always get up the same time, no matter when I get to bed. 'Bout five-thirty, quarter to six. Gotta get rollin', get the juices flowin', see what we've learned so we can lower the net on somebody."

"You about to lower the net on somebody?"

"Oh, yeah. I think we're closer than we've ever been in this case."

"You think Shannon did it, really?"

"What? Are you kidding? What do you think?"

"I don't think she did, Wally. I really don't."

"Well, neither do I."

"You don't?"

"'Course not. But don't tell her that. I need her on edge in case I'm wrong. I've been wrong before."

"You're not wrong this time."

"Well, I don't think I am either, kid, but let's not get over-confident."

"Who do you think did it?"

"Well, we all know it's gotta be somebody at that radio station. But you know what really threw me about this case at first?"

"Hm."

"The days of death."

"The *days* of death?"

"Yeah."

"I don't follow."

"Well, Ng was found on Wednesday and had been murdered on Tuesday. Matacena was found on Friday and had been murdered on Thursday. Of course, at that point I wasn't thinking about the days; I was thinking the way the reporters were thinking, that this killer had a thing about foreigners. Then Pritkin, a red-blooded American, is murdered on a Monday and I start wondering if this nut is going to try to rack up one for every day of the week. Not even three weeks later we find Jerome's body and the death day is set as Wednesday, OK? We've got Monday through Thursday so far, but not in that order. Now I'm betting that if another murder is committed, it's gonna be on a Friday. Four Fridays come and go and nothing. Then on Saturday, October 16, Frances Downs is found. The lab says she died on Friday.

"Now I live and die for Saturdays and Sundays, because while I've got no other leads except my nice-guy theory, I'm convinced we've got a calendar freak on our hands. Three weekends go by with nothing, and the creep surprises me with a Wednesday hit on Dr. McDough with a Thursday discovery. Shoots my theory sky high. I don't know what I was gonna do with that information anyway. I didn't stop any murders."

I yawned.

"You wanna get back home to bed, right?"

"No, no, Wally. I want to hear whatever you've got to say. I think this thing is going to be nudged around in your head until it all falls into place."

"Well, I had another theory that got blasted. After the first three, Ng, Matacena, and Pritkin, I was thinking we've got a murderer who can't stand poor people, right? I mean, when the preacher is the one with the most means of the three, you've got some poor people here, am I right?"

"Yeah."

"Yeah, but look at the next three. A lawyer, a kept woman who makes almost enough to keep herself, and a dentist. Three poor ones and three rich ones. What am I s'posed to do with that?"

"It must be nice to finally have a pattern that seems to make sense."

"Well, you're right, it does. But you know what I was saying to Shannon a little while ago made some sense too."

"That was scary. You sure convinced me you believed it."

"I convinced her too, didn't I? I wonder if she was starting to doubt herself and her own alibis there for a while. I'm tellin' ya, our psychologist woulda been proud of me."

"Were you proud of you?"

"You mean do I enjoy that, playin' district attorney? No. I'm good at it, and Merrill counts on me for it. You noticed how he played the soft and smooth role and I got to play the heavy? We do that a lot. I don't particularly enjoy it, but it has its place. I've surprised myself a few times with what I've dragged out of people."

"Were you surprised tonight?"

"Not really. She reacted the way an innocent person would react. Only a murderer guilty as sin would have looked me in the eye the first time around and said, 'No, sir, you're wrong.'"

Wally asked if I wanted to go somewhere for some dessert or something. I couldn't think of a worse suggestion, and I told him so.

"Well, then do you mind if I get something?"

"No, go ahead. I want to talk to you about something anyway."

"Uh-oh, here it comes."

"Here what comes? You don't know what I want to talk to you about."

"Don't I? You want me to write it on a piece of paper and see if I'm right?"

"Sure, go ahead."

And he did. He scribbled on one of his business cards and tucked it in his pocket. Then he drove down to the corner to an all-night diner where he ordered a big piece of pie with ice cream. I had ice water. "So, what do you wanna talk to me about?" he said.

"About having played a part in deceiving you today," I said.

"Oh, hey, forget it. I gave you a piece of my mind. I meant it. It was a lousy thing to do to a guy, but I can forget it. Why don't you?"

"I don't want to. I felt horrible about it all day, and I feel worse the more I think about it."

"Then don't think about it."

"How can I not think about it? You were so right, even when you were angry. I don't know when I've seen someone as mad, but you know you made sense. Every word made sense. You were beside yourself, yet your logic would have won any debate. You shot our reasons out of the water, and you convinced me that I had been part of a dirty deal."

"Good. That's all I wanted to do. I didn't want to put you so far under that you can't resurface. Come up for air, boy. It's over."

"Well, I want you to forgive me."

"I said I was forgetting it. What more do you want?"

"I want forgiveness. Sometimes forgetting glosses over forgiveness and there's still bitterness there deep down. Well, I can't blame you for the bitterness because of all the reasons you gave me when you were screaming at me. But I want you to forgive me, and if it's too early and the stench is too fresh in your mind, I can wait. I just want you to know I want to be forgiven and that I've learned a lesson."

For once, Wally Festschrift was at a loss for words. He

looked straight at me while shoveling down a couple of mammoth bites, then spoke. "That's real nice, Philip. You know, that really is. I think you mean what you're saying. You're not just trying to make yourself feel better. OK, then, I forgive you. On your terms. Forgetting *and* forgiving, no glossing over. No trying to say it wasn't as bad as it was or that there was some reason for it. Just plain old unconditional forgiveness. Good enough?"

"Good enough." And we shook hands.

"Well, you got me," he said as we went back to his car.

"I got you?"

"Yup. Here's what I wrote on the card."

It read: *Preaching. Just like Earl.*

I laughed. "I'm glad you brought that up," I said.

"Oh, no."

"C'mon, you *want* to talk about it, I can tell."

"You can, huh? How can you tell?

"You brought it up, didn't you?"

"Yeah, I guess I did."

"You know, you brought it up last time too."

"I did?"

"Yeah. You came right out and asked me what my philosophy of life is or something like that."

"I remember that."

"So, what did Earl talk to you about?"

"You know."

"Well, I know what he told us, but I don't know what you thought of it."

"I thought it was strange. You know, it was the last thing I expected to hear from Earl. 'Course it would be even more surprising to hear something like that from an old coot like me, but Earl is so self-sufficient and smooth."

"Don't I know it."

"I s'pose. But he was givin' it to me with both barrels.

And he wasn't trying to say he was better than me either. That's what I thought was so weird. He was telling me that I needed God in my life and that God can be personal and all that through Jesus Christ. Well, it sounded pretty good. He was giving me all the unconditional love business about forgiving my past and making something out of what was left of my life, even with all my failures. He made it sound pretty attractive and simple. I told him I didn't see myself as a church-goin' type, and he said the same went for him. But you know what he said? He said he thought one day he probably was going to take the step, be a Christian, start going to church and the whole thing."

"He said that?"

"Sure as you're sittin' there."

"How did you react?"

"I told him if he did, I would."

"But he didn't?"

"Not yet. I was going to talk to him about it, but there hasn't been time, and we lost contact up until today."

"You know, Wally, what he decides really has nothing to do with what you decide."

"I know that. You know, a funny thing happened though, when it was all over and we had gone our separate ways. I quit smoking."

"I noticed that, but what did that have to do with what Earl was talking about?"

"I'm not sure. I said something about my smoking while he was preaching at me, and he insisted that smoking had nothing to do with it. He kept harpin' on the fact that it had nothing to do with my doing good things or not doing bad things, it was all what God could do for me if I'd let Him. I got the point, I mean I really did. The fact that I can remember it now tells me that I got the point real good. But for some reason, I decided I wanted to quit smoking after all these years, and I did. It wasn't easy, but I did it. Something about just having talked with Earl about all that stuff made me feel better about myself or something, and I just found the strength I never had to quit."

"What made you feel so good about what he had said?"

"I guess it was just the idea that God might really love ol' Wally Festschrift after all. That I was worth something to somebody, even Earl, after everything. And if there's anything to it, and if I do someday take the step Earl might take, well, at the time I felt good about that."

"And how do you feel about it now?"

# TEN

"Right now I feel tired about it," Festschrift said.

"So do I, and I don't want to push you, Wally," I said, "but if you don't want to talk about it, you can just tell me. You don't have to blame it on fatigue."

"I'm not, kid. Really I'm not. In fact I *want* to talk about it some more, maybe with you *and* Earl. I wouldn't even mind showin' up at your church there with you and your fiancée. 'S long as Earl will come too."

"Margo and I would love that, but she's not my fiancée."

"She's not?"

"We're not officially engaged."

"Well, what're you waitin' for? She's a terrific girl. Smart too."

"Oh, I know. I'm waiting for her to finish waiting for me."

"You'll have to explain that one."

"Well, she asked for time the last time we were engaged and I got huffy and almost dumped her. Now she's all grown up and mature—I mean she really is; it's amazing how she's changed since then. Anyway, I think it's given her unusual insight into me. Whether I think it or not, *she* does."

"Does what? Have insight or think she does?"

"Both. And I think she feels she has a better idea than I do of when I'm really going to be ready for a lifetime commitment. I disagree with her on the surface. I love her and feel I'm ready. But I have a nagging fear. More like respect really. I'm so afraid that she might be right that I'm not pushing her. It's not like she's acting like we're *not* going to be engaged again."

"And you're not gonna push me either—on this church thing I mean?"

"'Course not, Wally. That's the last thing I'd want to do. But, you know, I had a young friend I was careful not to push and he committed suicide before I ever really got to the point with him. And when you really believe what you're talking about is a life or death matter, that hurts."

"Ouch. I'll bet it did. But I'll tell you what, I'm not even considering suicide."

"I know, but who knows what could happen? An accident, a heart attack."

"Hey, don't start with me. The only worry I have about heart attacks is when my friends double deal me."

"Guilty. I thought you'd forgotten and forgiven."

"You're right. I have. Tell you what, let's make a deal. The Sunday after we solve this murder case, I'll talk ol' Earl into goin' to church. We'll make it a foursome."

"It's a deal, but you're in trouble now. When I tell Margo, she'll start praying that it'll happen this week, and when she starts praying, things start happening."

"I'm all for that. I'll be prayin' the same way. This case has got to break soon, kid."

I opened the door and walked around to my car. Wally started his and rolled his window all the way down. "Listen, Philip. I don't want to lead you on or anything. What I mean is, I don't want you to get your hopes up about me, or even Earl for that matter. I don't mind talkin' to you about this stuff, and that's more'n I can say for the way I was when we first met. But just don't read too much into it. There's a lot of water over my dam, and some things just never change. OK?"

I wanted to argue with him, but he wasn't in the mood. I knew of worse characters than Wally Festschrift who'd been changed by God. But I just nodded, he touched his fingers to his forehead in a little salute, and we drove off.

I was telling Margo all about it in the office early the next afternoon when Earl called everybody into his office and asked Larry to see if Shannon could join us. As is Earl's custom, he didn't say a word until everyone was in and seated.

He interlocked his fingers, tucked them under his chin, and rested his elbows on the desk in front of him. "Chicago Homicide has been busy this morning," he began. "They have a plan, and I like it. They have done some undercover checking on your alibis, Shannon, and they feel fairly confident that you can be used to lure the murderer out into the open."

"Does that mean they believe me now?"

"If they still had doubts, I don't think they'd let you out of their—or our—sight."

"Well, I'm relieved, but are you sure they aren't just trying to set *me* up? Are you sure they don't still believe I'm guilty and are just trying to put me in a position to prove it?"

"I know how you could feel that way after last night," Earl said, "but they've done their homework today and now they agree with us that though it's unlikely you are involved with the murders, no doubt you are either a target or the catalyst."

"It's *unlikely* I'm involved? Is that all you can say?"

Larry broke in. "Shannon, surely you know by now that we all know you're innocent. Earl is trying to emphasize that you are also in the middle of this thing. Have you let that sink in? All these grisly murders that have been in the news every day for months have revolved around you."

"I thought of that first, remember? And I'm sorry. I know you all believe me or you wouldn't have taken care of me so well. I'm not sure I want to be involved in luring any killer out though."

"Think about this," Margo said. "We're all pretty sure the murderer is not only someone you know, but also someone you work with who must have some sort of a morbid fascination with you. It's time to start thinking who that might be. It may seem unfair to lay that responsibility on you, and you can shirk it if you want to, but why not seize the moment? How much better to grit your teeth for a few more days for the sake of saving more people."

No one said anything for a moment until Earl spoke. "Well, Margo, you took the words right out of Lieutenant Merrill's mouth. In effect, that's what he told me on the phone this morning. He wasn't quite so eloquent, but you've read him well on their view of Shannon's role. They'd like us to meet with their psychologist, a woman named Dr. Mary Stone from International University. They've been feeding her all the information they have, virtually everything that pertains. And now they want you to tell her what you can about your office, the people you work with, your relationships, everything. Are you willing?"

"Of course."

The five of us met with Dr. Stone, Merrill, and Festschrift in a hotel room in the south suburbs. A stack of computer readouts lay before Dr. Stone, and she had taken copious notes. As we arrived several plainclothesmen were leaving. "You're last on the docket today," Wally said as his eyes met Shannon's. "We've never had this many men on one case. Dr. Stone has all the information except yours." Shannon appeared not to be listening. Wally put his hand in front of her and she slowed. "Miss Perry, please. I know you're upset with me. Let me explain."

"There's no need," she said, her tone cold. "I know you were doing your job." She tried to walk past him but he put his hand gently on her shoulder. She looked impatient but she didn't pull away.

"Hey, I sometimes hate that part of my job," he said. "You've gotta understand that."

"You didn't appear to hate it last night."

"That's all part of doing it right. I'm sorry if I hurt you. Will you believe that?"

"I'll try."

We were all introduced to Dr. Stone, a handsome woman in a tweed suit who appeared slightly detached, as if she had just crammed for a test and didn't want to run into anything for fear she would lose half of what she had stored in her mind. Indeed that was the case, she admitted. "I need to tie the loose ends of all this information together so I can make some sense of it," she said. "And perhaps I can offer something useful. If you're ready, Miss Perry, I'd like to just ask you several questions."

"I'm ready, and please call me Shannon."

"All right, Shannon. I want you to tell me about the office where you work. It's a radio station and you're a newswriter, I know that. Tell me about the physical layout and the people, and please sketch the floor plan on this board as you talk."

"I'm not much of an artist," Shannon said. Standing beside the two-foot by three-foot chalkboard with chalk in hand, she began to sketch a large square. "The office is here in the back. Basically we're in one big room with little offices around the perimeter. The office coordinator and an assistant newswriter and a part-time secretary have their desks together in the middle of the open area and my office is here. Then here's the entrance to the control room and the booth beyond it. Then on the other side of the entrance here is my boss's office and workshop."

"Thank you, that's good," the doctor said. "Put names with these people please, just first names if you wish."

"Could I ask a question first?" Earl said. "How far is it here between your office and your boss's office?"

"The doorways would be about ten feet apart."

"And it appears you can see each other if you want to, while each of you is in his own office I mean."

"Right."

"Do I see three doors on your boss's office?"

"Yes, Jake can come into the large office area, go into the control room, or into the workshop."

"I'm sorry," Earl said, "can I ask just one more? What happens in the workshop?"

"Oh, all the equipment repair, storage for extra mikes and remote equipment, that kind of thing. Our part-time sound man, Steve—he's about nineteen—spends most of his time in there when he's not in the control room. Jake does a lot of maintenance work on the equipment too."

"The boss does?" Earl pressed.

"Oh, yes. We're a small station. Everybody does double

duty. I even have to take my turn as receptionist, and I'm making union scale as a newswriter."

"I'm sorry, Doctor," Earl said.

"It's quite all right, sir." Dr. Stone said. "If there's one thing I'm fairly confident about in this case, it's that we're dealing with a volatile individual who is increasing the rapidity with which he or she commits violent acts. Anything you notice or need that will help us locate this individual, please feel free to mention.

"Now, Shannon, the office coordinator is?"

"Betty."

"And your relationship with her?"

"Strictly business. Never social. We get along very well. She likes me, I think."

"Any doubts?"

"No, in fact, people have told me that she says nice things about me, which is the best kind of compliment."

"And the assistant writer . . ."

"Is Jeanie. We're friends. Not close because she works for me, but we do see each other socially. I don't confide in her or anything, although I think she'd like me to. Sometimes she tells me personal things, but lately she hasn't. It's probably because I haven't told her my secrets."

"Do you think that bothers Jeanie?"

"Oh, not really."

"Do you think she has any grudges against you, any jealousies? Could she hate you or have any reason to get back at you for anything?"

"I'd be surprised if she did. We've had some minor arguments and a few hurt feelings over the past two years. She had a little trouble adjusting to me as her supervisor because when she finished college she thought she was ready to take over for Dan Rather. But I think I've taught her some things along the way."

"Does she think so?"

"She wouldn't admit it in so many words, but yes, I think she knows I've been good to her and fair with her. The only problem she has with me is that I don't gossip. She loves to talk about people, and I love to listen. But I won't do it myself."

"Does this bother her?"

"You mean enough to make her do something terrible? No."

"Since she works for you, you are responsible for her hours and so forth?"

"Yes."

"Has she had any unusual absences, or is she usually there during the normal business day?"

"Well, we all are. Yes, she's always there. The only people with irregular hours are the secretary, Debbie, and then the on-air people who work a couple of hours before and a couple of hours after their shifts on the air. For instance Chuck works four A.M. to noon but is on the air only from six to ten. Steve is going to school, so he works mornings. And Jake works eight to noon and four to eight."

"Why those hours for Jake? You said he was the boss?"

"Right. It puts him in the office for the sake of the office staff and he also catches, let's see, half of four different DJs' shows."

"Is he ever there in the afternoons?"

"Oh, yes. Sometimes he'll save some of his shop work for his off time. I think he does some work on his own stereo equipment there too."

"Does that bother anyone?"

"Oh, no. Nothing Jake does could bother anyone."

"How do you mean? And while you're answering that, explain as carefully as you can, your relationship with him."

"I was in awe of him at first. Everyone is. He's been around. He was a big rock DJ in a couple of big markets in the sixties."

"Do you know where?" Lieutenant Merrill asked.

"Both coasts I think. L.A. or San Diego and then Baltimore I believe. And he's an impressive guy. He's very good looking, tall, a wide-open face, naturally curly blond hair, wears those big glasses. And he's really nice too."

"Excuse me," Margo said. "Earl, I've been listening for some connection with this S.D. inscription on the shell casings. Shannon, do you know what Steve's middle name is? You said his last name was Lacey, I believe."

"Yes, and I do know his middle name because we kid him about his initials spelling S-O-L, *sun* in Spanish. His middle name is Owen."

"OK, and then you mentioned that Jake was a DJ in San Diego. Los Angeles is called L.A.; is San Diego ever called S.D.?"

"I'll check on it right now, " Wally said, rising. "My guys have been investigating Childers anyway, and I want their input too. It shouldn't be too hard to trace Jake Raven to San Diego if he ever worked there."

"Ask his agency," Shannon said. "Farrar on Michigan Avenue."

"He's got an agency?"

"He still does emceeing and grand openings and stuff life that. He's a real professional. We've all learned a lot from him."

"I'm also gonna check on this Lacey kid's attendance at his afternoon classes on the days of the murders. The coroner has pretty much concluded that they were all afternoon jobs, committed by someone who studied the victims' patterns and knew when they would be home."

Dr. Stone stood and paced, questioning Shannon for almost another hour. "Please go back to your relationship with Jake. Is everyone so enamored of him?"

"Yes. He's really quite special. He has high standards and he gets the best out of everyone, but I don't think he has ever hurt anyone. He can correct you, even criticize you, and make you feel good about it. He never puts anyone down, seems to be fairly close to everyone at work, but he's divorced and lives alone."

"I understand you dated him a few times."

"Well, not really. We thought up reasons to sort of go out together, but they weren't official dates. One was to the wedding, and once was a dinner to celebrate my anniversary with the station. Very casual. I don't think I would have gone out with him if he had asked me for a real date. For one thing he was only recently divorced, and come to think of it, he did ask me out after his divorce was final. That was sort of to celebrate that. See? Always reasons, not real dates. I just wouldn't feel comfortable dating my boss. Not just because he's my boss, but because I really do kind of have him on a pedestal. He's in his early forties, and, no, I wouldn't actually date him for real."

"How does he feel about that?"

"He kidded me about it a few times, said I was rejecting him or something. He's a cutup. He did that in front of people. Of course, he never really asked me out for a date-type date. But I think he knows I wouldn't accept anyway. I really wouldn't. It would scare me to death."

Wally returned. "Have you talked about Childers yet?"

"No, we were just getting to him," the doctor said.

"Has anything hit you yet with the others?"

"This Jeanie could have some latent hostility for Shannon and I'm a little fuzzy on the student, but I don't think there's anything else here so far."

"Well, the student, Steve, has perfect attendance in his

afternoon classes except he was absent one week when he was at his parents' home, and that checks out."

Dr. Stone, who had added first names to the office positions listed on the board, leaned over and X'd Steve's name off.

"But we've gotta talk about Childers," Wally said.

"Chuck Childers. When I asked the agency if Jake Raven had ever worked out of San Diego, they said no. L.A., Pittsburgh, and Baltimore before Chicago. Never San Diego. But you know what they said? They said, 'You must be thinking about the guy who works for Raven, the morning man.'

"I said. 'Yeah?'

"And they said, 'Yeah, he was the biggest thing to hit San Diego in years before he went to Oklahoma City.'"

We all looked at each other.

"I knew he was in Oklahoma City, but he never told me he worked in California," Shannon said.

"You dated him for how long?" Dr. Stone said.

"For about a year, up until May or so."

"And he never told you he had lived in California?"

Shannon shook her head, her eyes tearing.

"There's something else he didn't tell you, Shannon," Wally said. "My boys have reason to believe he's the guy who'd been paying Frances Downs's rent for the last two years."

# ELEVEN

Shannon pressed her hands to her temples and closed her eyes. Dr. Stone put a hand on Shannon's knee. "We're going to have to talk about this."

Shannon nodded, grimacing, her eyes still shut. "Not Chuck, no, please not Chuck. Even after we broke up, I confided in Chuck. He knew everything about me."

"Even who your dentist was?" Festschrift asked.

"Of course. We went together. We were nearly engaged."

"Were you intimate with him?"

Shannon nodded. "I never lived with him or anything like that, but yes."

"Did he tell you he was divorced?"

"Yes."

"It's not true," Wally said. "He's separated, but he is not divorced. He has two children in Oklahoma City."

Shannon covered her eyes with her hand. "He said he never had children."

Dr. Stone brushed off her skirt and crossed her arms. "What would you gentlemen like to do? You can, of course, pick him up in connection with the Downs murder, I imagine. Do we need carry this any further?"

"We still don't have a motive," Merrill said.

"Of course you do," Dr. Stone said. "She broke up with him, right? Rejection. Humiliation. Revenge."

"But why all the little people in her life? It still doesn't add up," Wally said.

"Anyway," Lieutenant Merrill broke in, "I don't want this guy on one suspicion of murder if I can get him on six. He sounds like a first class lowlife, but lying about your marital status is no crime unless you're guilty of bigamy. You didn't marry the guy, did you?"

Shannon shook her head.

"And there's no law says you can't pay a woman's rent, either. He was likely guilty of adultery—well, we know that—but we're not on vice detail. If this is the guy and he's as volatile as you say, Doctor, let's find out what sets him off and then let's set him off. Tell Shannon what it is she's doin' that makes him do what he does, and then we'll catch him in the act."

Shannon was shaking her head. She looked like she might get hysterical. Margo spoke to her. "Honey, listen, I know you're still finding it hard to believe this guy would lie to you and cheat on you and then act this way just because you wanted out of the relationship, but think about what he's done to you and to other innocent people. Can't you consider doing whatever you need to, to stop him?"

Shannon ran to the bathroom, and we could hear her sobbing for several minutes. Dr. Stone conferred with Merrill while the rest of us fidgeted. Margo walked over to me, oblivious to the others in the room, and wearily put her head on my chest and wrapped her arms around me. "Bizarre," she said quietly.

We all fell silent when Shannon reappeared. "I'm ready

to do whatever I have to do," she said "But can it wait until tomorrow?"

Dr. Stone looked at the lieutenant.

"The actual work can wait, but we'll need to set it all in motion today. I want Dr. Stone to determine what it is you say or do that pushes this guy over the edge. Then I want you to call your boss and thank him for the time off and tell him you're better and you want to come back to work. Then you work on Childers and we'll keep him in sight every minute."

"I think I can help you even more," Dr. Stone said. "I believe that perhaps this man can be programmed to go after someone specific. Would that help?"

"Would that *help?* You bet it would! If we can use some bait and stake out the place where we think he's heading, we'll have him red-handed."

"Well, no matter who we try to set him up for, you'd better protect Shannon too, because I think he's leading up to her. I'm guessing that her propensity for talking up these minor characters in her life whom she sees as so wonderful drives him crazy. In his mind, if he can do away with all these selfless people, he will have no competition left. Yet this man knows himself. Imagine how many people he will have to destroy before he's the best one left."

"If that's true, then isn't Jake vulnerable, too?" Merrill asked.

"Do you talk about Jake at work the way you did here today?" Dr. Stone asked.

"Well, no, not really. Everyone pretty much feels the same about Jake. Even Chuck. It's sort of a given. No one says much. I've said it to Jake of course, but Chuck and I haven't talked about Jake that much."

"But you have, as you think back on it now, said complimentary things about these people, all six of them, to Chuck?"

"Yes. All of them. The thing is, he must be a great con man. In spite of all I'm finding out now about Chuck, he always agrees with me when I say good things about people. I can't believe it's all an act. I just can't believe it."

"I'd still like to know how he gets into people's homes and makes them trust him to the point where he can murder them with no signs of struggle," Merrill said.

"He's a charmer," Shannon said. "He could talk you into anything."

"I want to be the bait," Larry said suddenly. "I want this creep."

"Oh, hey, I don't know . . ." Earl said.

"Me either," Merrill said. "We've got plenty of undercover cops who can play a role."

"No, maybe he's onto something here," Wally said. "Larry's a natural because it's for real. Shannon can truthfully say that this guy has been very nice to her lately. When she was distraught over personal matters, he helped her. It's perfect."

"I agree," Dr. Stone said. "I mean, it's not my place to suggest such specific detail, but I do know it will help Shannon if she can be telling the truth even when she knows she's playacting for a purpose. It will be easier for her."

Shannon stared at Larry. "Larry, you've become very special to me these last few days. I can't think of risking your life."

"You can't talk me out of it, Shannon. You don't deserve something like this. I want to do it and I'm going to."

Dr. Stone raised a brow at Merrill. "I believe it is up to you, sir."

Merrill looked at Earl. "Wally is apparently for it. How about you?"

"Aah," Earl said. "I don't know. I don't like it much, but we're going to make it airtight, aren't we? Heavy stake-outs? People hidden within a few feet of Larry all the time?"

"Of course," Merrill said. "Larry, if you're willing to sign a few releases and your boss frees you to do it, I can pay you one day's patrolman's wages."

Larry looked at Earl, who shrugged. "Why not? You've done crazier things."

Shannon and Dr. Stone spent another hour carefully going over the way Shannon would act in the office. "It's important that you try to return to normal, at least to the level of normalcy you were at last week. The key is to continue to say good things about people, especially Mr. Shipman."

"That's right," Lieutenant Merrill said. "Make it natural. Tell whoever you would normally tell that Larry has been so kind to you."

"See, I know Chuck," Larry said. "It would be the most natural thing in the world for Shannon to talk about me in the office. I'm sort of a regular around the place anyway. I get in there every few weeks or so."

"Did Chuck tell *you* he's worked in San Diego?" Shannon asked.

"No, I thought he'd gotten his start in a small station in Oklahoma and then moved to the big one in Oklahoma City before coming here. I gotta tell ya, though, it doesn't terribly surprise me about his relationship with Frances. I thought about warning you a few times how he talked about women, but about the time I really thought I should, you broke up with him anyway."

"Was that a traumatic break?" the doctor wanted to know.

"Well, it was for me, but Chuck was so good about it. I can see why, now. Jake was wonderful too. He was upset with Chuck for a while, assuming Chuck must have hurt me in some way, but that wasn't it. I was just feeling crowded, and I was uncomfortable carrying on a relationship with someone I worked with."

"Was there any one thing that brought about the break?"

"Not really. He did want me to move in with him, but I just couldn't. As I told you, I'm not a prude, but I haven't gone quite that far astray from the way I was raised."

"Was he upset?"

"Disappointed. He acted hurt for a while, but he agreed we could still be friends and that he wouldn't hold a grudge. It was an item of conversation around the station for a week or so, but it's been since May now and I thought it was finished. I really did."

"You still talk with Chuck a lot, like you used to?"

"That's just it. More than ever. I didn't talk to him about what's been troubling me lately because I was embarrassed. I thought I was going crazy and that everyone was seeing all the coincidences like I was. But we talked every day."

"What did you say about Jake's being upset with Chuck?"

"I told him I really thought Chuck was being nice about it and to please let it blow over. They've always had a good relationship. Jake hired Chuck, you know, and he's proud of him. We all are. Were anyway."

"Do Chuck and Jake socialize together?"

"No, not much. Jake tells his people that he'll go with them in a group, but that his policy is that he can't favor any over the others away from the office."

"But he wanted to favor you."

"Oh, that was just to cheer me up after I broke up with

Chuck. It was hard for me for a while, but Jake was so nice. They both were."

"And even though they don't socialize away from work, they're on good terms?"

"They must be."

"Why's that?"

"Because Jake often talks to me about things I discuss with Chuck. He'll bring them up and I'll just know it's something I talked to Chuck about but not to Jake. I talk to them both, like I say, but there are differences in the things we talk about. I'm a little more personal with Chuck, naturally."

"Does it bother you that Chuck shares these things with Jake?"

"Chuck denies it. He says I must have told Jake and didn't remember, but I'm not that dumb. I told Jake once that I wasn't so sure I liked Chuck telling him what I talk about, and he tried to make me believe that I had told him too."

"Where does all this talking go on, at a lunchroom or something?"

"No, Chuck doesn't go anywhere but straight into the studio and then either to Jake's office or the workshop or home. I talk to him during the music when he's on the air. Unless Jake can read lips—his office is in the line through the studio window, but of course, the studio is sound-proof—I can't see how he can tell what we talk about if Chuck isn't telling him."

"Why would Chuck tell him?"

"I don't know. It's nothing big. I don't bad-mouth any-one. I guess it isn't even worth worrying about, but you can imagine how it makes me feel. It isn't often, you know, but once in a while Jake just happens to mention some-thing I know I haven't talked to him about and I somehow feel as if Chuck has betrayed me. It's like my privacy has been invaded. Oh, it's no big thing."

"Yes, it is," Dr. Stone said. "It's a very natural reaction. Frankly I don't know how it fits into the picture I'm getting of Chuck Childers, but in a way it says something interesting about Jake, doesn't it? Sometimes we're tempted to tell someone that we know something about them that they don't know we know. However he's getting the information—apparently from Chuck for some reason, who may be subtly showing off to Jake that he's still close enough to you to hear personal information—Jake is possibly trying to say, by repeating it, that he is concerned with your personal life too. He may want to convince you that you were the one who told him, in the hope that you will bring him into that kind of relationship."

"But I just talk about things like when I get my car fixed or when my mother is coming to town or when a check bounces. Those aren't the kinds of things you tell Jake, or any boss, I imagine."

"That doesn't negate my point," Dr. Stone said, smiling. "In fact, it's the very type of thing Jake would want you to tell him if he's more interested in you than you think."

"Oh, I doubt it."

"Could it be he's getting this type of information from one of the girls in the office?"

Shannon thought for a moment. "Well, I tell more of it to Chuck than to anyone, but I suppose it's possible. I doubt it, though. That's just not the kind of thing anyone talks to Jake about, and sometimes the period between when I've mentioned something to Chuck and when I hear it from Jake is so short that I just know Chuck is the big mouth."

Festschrift stood and looked at his watch. "I don't want to rush you, but it's after four and Jake should be back in the office. Shannon should call and tell him she wants to come back to work tomorrow."

"I think we're through," Dr. Stone said. "Anything else you want to tell me, Shannon?"

"Just a question. How am I supposed to feel about this? I feel guilty already, playacting and pretending. Plus I'm bitter toward Chuck."

"That's understandable. Calm yourself as much as possible and remind yourself of the terror this city is going through. You have a chance to do something about that. This man has lied to you. It's not unfair for you to avenge that by stopping him from what he's doing."

"Sergeant Festschrift, what should I say to Jake?"

"Tell him you're sorry about your work lately and that you have just been overtired. Promise to do your best work and all that."

While Shannon was waiting for an answer at the station, Festschrift began gathering information from Larry about the location and floor plan of his apartment. "I'm gonna want to see that tonight and spend the night there. We'll decide who'll be stationed where, and I think four of us should be able to handle it, inside and out."

"Hello, Debbie," Shannon said, and we were all silent, "this is Shannon. . . . Hi, fine. . . . No, in fact I think I'll probably be in tomorrow. . . . No, just tired, you know. Is Jake around? . . . Thanks."

Shannon's hands shook, but resolve was written in her face. "Hi, Jake. Listen, I think I want to come in tomorrow. . . . No, I'm OK, really. I was just overtired and I feel a lot better since I rested over the weekend and today." She held up her crossed fingers and we smiled. "No, I appreciate that, but I'd just as soon come back to work. I'm going crazy here." There was truth to that. She made a face as if he was insisting that she stay away a few more days. "Really, Jake, a friend, well, you know Larry Shipman? Yeah. He's kind of taken me under his wing and I feel better now, so unless you're going to lock me out, I'll plan on being there tomorrow at eight. . . . No, I wouldn't if I weren't sure I am ready. I'll be my old self, and if I'm not, you can send me home, I promise. OK, Jake? . . . Thanks. I'll see you tomorrow."

She hung up and flopped into a chair. "I thought I wasn't going to be able to talk him into it!" she said. "I must have done really lousy work last week! He's so sweet. He kept saying that they missed me but that he didn't want me to come back until I was sure I was ready and not to feel pressure or feel obligated or anything. It was almost like he didn't want me to come back!" But the look on her face made it clear that he had convinced her of the opposite and that he was just watching out for her. She was still obviously nervous about the next day, but she was pleased too.

# TWELVE

Dr. Stone shook hands all around and tucked her leather folder under her arm. At the door she turned. "Shannon, I'll be thinking of you tomorrow. If you talk to Chuck Childers as easily and naturally as you just talked to your boss—and if you even use pretty much the same words—we'll know soon enough if he's our man."

Lieutenant Merrill said she should even act embarrassed and noncommittal if anyone asked—as they surely would—whether there was anything going on between her and Larry. He insisted that the most important part, and they rehearsed it several times, was that she should mention that she wished she had taken off one more day because Larry was off all day Tuesday. "You might even ask if you can leave a half-hour early, even though you hate to ask Jake because you talked him into letting you come back before you needed to."

They ran through a few role plays, interrupted only when Shannon wondered aloud if she was up to it. But a pep talk from Margo and Wally helped her begin to warm to the idea that she could kill two birds with the same stone. She could protect society while repaying Childers for his deceitfulness.

Shannon provided Lieutenant Merrill with photos of the people in her office. Chicago Homicide arranged for a stakeout of her apartment, where she would spend the night and then report to work as usual. Margo was asked to be in on that surveillance while Earl would work with Lieutenant Merrill outside Larry's apartment building and would alert Wally and me inside when anyone was coming. "I wouldn't have chosen you first necessarily," Wally told me, "but the way Larry describes that utility closet in his kitchen, it sounds like you'll be the only one who can fit between the water heater and the washer/dryer."

Just to be safe, all the squad cars were exchanged for personal cars and the stakeouts were set to begin early that evening. It was unlikely anyone was onto us, but even if they were, they wouldn't have looked for us to start getting into place the night before when we didn't expect any action until the following afternoon.

Those of us on the Shipman detail grabbed some fast food and ate at Larry's little kitchen table. "Wally, this is up to you," Merrill said, "but since the kitchen is right off the entrance here and the dining room is out of sight off the kitchen, I would think you'd want to be in the dining room and Philip in this closet, as you say. With that closet light off, Philip will be able to see out through the crack between the louvered doors without Childers seeing in. We want him in the process of doing whatever it is he does, and then you should take him. If he's just talking or going through some ritual, that's one thing. When he gets to the point of putting a gun in his hand, don't wait."

"Please," Larry said. "Don't wait."

Lieutenant Merrill continued. "Wally will be just around the passageway from the dining room in the kitchen; that's why it's important for you to steer him into the kitchen, because if he gets into the living room, he'll be able to see Wally in the dining room."

Earl wedged himself in the closet where I would be the next afternoon. "I could almost do it, but if I sneezed I'd blow the water heater."

Everyone laughed except me. "I'll be within three feet of Larry and Childers standing there," I said. "Won't he be able to hear me breathe?"

"You won't be breathing," Earl said, and again everyone but me was laughing. Earl turned serious. "You know, Philip, if anything goes wrong, you'll know first. If he should grab that gun and start waving it around or trying to force Larry to stand somewhere, you haven't time to call for help. Maybe Wally will hear enough to make him come in immediately; maybe he won't. You'll be able to see everything, and if you have a doubt in your mind, you've got to drop him."

"You mean . . . ?"

"You know what I mean." He shut the closet door and turned the light off. I heard him empty the bullets from his snub-nosed revolver and drop them into his pants pocket. "That's the one thing I'm doing that you won't do," he said. "Now I'm standing here with my gun in my right hand, my arm is bent at the elbow, and the gun is pressed to my chest, just under my chin. Keep your eyes on me."

There was nothing to see. The closet was dark. Even though we knew he was in there, it almost seemed as if he weren't. We waited several seconds, no one moving, all eyes on the door. We jumped when it burst open and Earl stood there, arm extended as if it had all happened in one motion, his gun to my head.

I let out a sigh.

"But you don't come out of there unless you mean to

drop the man," he said. "That means you're kicking the door and firing at his head in the same motion, probably two shots as fast as you can because you're not making this move unless he has the three fifty-seven in his hand. Until he does, you stay put. Ideally, Wally should enter and you should come out slowly at about the same time, just before the man actually raises the weapon. That's much cleaner, and you'll avoid having to kill a man."

I stood quickly and walked into the living room, suddenly overheated and short of breath. Pulling back the curtains, I pressed my forehead against the cool glass of Larry's eighth-floor picture window and pretended to study the Chicago traffic below. I half expected Earl to come and give me one of his famous welcome-to-the-big-leagues pep talks, but he didn't. In fact, no one at the table said a word as Earl sat back down.

I wasn't sure I was ready to kill a man, justified or not. It wasn't a moral issue. A man who has killed six people in cold blood should be shot on the spot if he is standing with his gun pointed at victim number seven. I just didn't know if I was cut out to do it. I had thought that if someone came into the apartment with a gun in his pocket, we could just grab him and take him in and hope we had the right gun, the etched shell, and enough of the rest of the pieces of the M.O. to make it stick. And we probably could have. But with the crazy legal loopholes and the restrictions put on law enforcement people these days, it's always better to catch your criminals in the act.

I sat on the couch and folded my hands in my lap, letting my head fall back. I stared at the ceiling. "You wanna get in on a game of cards, Philip?" Larry called out.

"Nah," I said, my voice sounding strange because of the position of my neck. "You guys feel free." I wouldn't have known how anyway, but that wasn't the whole problem and Larry knew it. I heard some quiet talk. Then Larry came in and sat next to me.

"Wanna talk?" he said.

"Not really."

"Wanna listen?"

"OK."

"I just want to give you my perspective on this," he said. "I appreciate you and your straight life and your beliefs and all that. I really do. I think you and Margo are special people. But let me be a little selfish here for a minute. Let me think of me and my neck.

"I volunteered for this assignment. I mean, I made 'em let me do it. I don't mind tellin' you, it scares me. I'm not backing out, but I want you to if you don't think you can protect me. If something, anything, makes you hesitate when you should be acting, I'm a dead man. Don't let anyone shame you into this, Philip. You gotta go into it with full confidence that you'll do whatever you have to do. You don't have to like it, but you've got to do it. Otherwise, tell us now so we can get some other skinny little guy to stand in the closet."

He slapped me on the knee and went back to the kitchen. I started to pray about it, then I realized the unique nature of the prayer. I had never asked God for the kind of courage this would take, and it took me a while to settle it in my head. Was I asking for the strength, the courage, the ability to be an agent of death? Or of justice? I confess I was not exactly awash in any peace borne of a commitment to justifiable homicide, but after a few minutes I did rise and shakily retake my seat in the kitchen. "I'll do it and I'll be ready," I said, looking at the floor.

No one responded. I watched them play a slow, somber, unspirited game of cards until almost two o'clock in the morning. Before Merrill and Earl left, the lieutenant gave his last bit of instruction. "Shannon will call us when Childers leaves the office tomorrow, and it will be radioed to me. I'll radio it to Wally up here. I don't want her or anyone else calling here because a busy phone could scare off our man. And remember, nine out of ten stakeouts are just long waits for nothing. Shannon's going to do everything she can to let Chuck know that Larry is home today, but who can know the mind of a madman? He might not be ready to move for another week or two."

"On the other hand," a weary Sergeant Festschrift said, "he just might be ready tomorrow."

"That's why we're here," Merrill said.

The sergeant and I stretched out in the living room, but I can't say I slept much. Wally snored some, but every few hours he would sigh and move about. I got the impression Larry wasn't having an easy night either.

In the morning we freshened up a bit without shaving and sat around small-talking and letting our beards grow. At about ten Lieutenant Merrill called on a special frequency on Wally's walkie-talkie. It sounded strange that they didn't have to use code numbers. "Hey Wally, come in."

"Yeah, boss."

"We just got a call from Shannon. She feels pretty good about how it's going. She told Chuck she might ask Jake if she could get off a little early because Larry was off today, but she had hardly been back at her desk for two minutes when Jake buzzed her and asked if she could work late because he's expecting some wire service guys to come in at four-thirty. What do you make of that?"

"Sounds legit. She'll keep us informed when Childers leaves work at midday?"

"Yeah. This Steve kid isn't working today. Exams or something."

"Thanks, boss."

"Something else, Wally. Childers asked Shannon a few questions about Larry. Like does he enjoy his work and what does he really do with the agency, stuff like that."

Wally didn't answer.

"You get that, Wally?"

"Yeah. I don't know what to think."

"We don't talk about it much, now that I think about it," Larry told Wally. "He knows I work at EH but that's all. He never asked for details."

Wally nodded. "Lieutenant?"

"Yeah."

"We don't know if that means anything. We're out."

"Merrill over and out."

"I'll bet the sound from that studio is piped into Jake Raven's office," Larry said, almost to himself.

Festschrift was antsy now. I was just quiet.

"You guys wanna watch some TV or something?" Larry said. "This is like waitin' for Christmas."

"Not exactly," I said.

"Well, not exactly, no, but the time is draggin'."

"Sure," Wally said. "I'm up for a little TV."

We must have been a sight, lounging in Larry's living room watching game shows that marked the half hours with panels and prizes and celebrity guests and commercials. At eleven-thirty the phone rang. Wally jumped up and turned the TV off. "Take it in the kitchen. We'll listen in out here."

We were in direct sight of the kitchen phone, so Wally put his hand on the receiver and signaled Larry when to answer. Wally and I pressed our faces together so we could both hear.

"Hello, this is Shipman."

"Hi, Larry. You recognize my voice, don't you?"

"Yeah . . ."

"Don't say my name. There are some things I'd like to talk to you about in light of your line of work, and I'd rather not discuss them by phone."

"OK." Larry nodded vigorously to indicate that it was Childers. "What do you want to do?"

"Well, listen, you know the girl I was going with for a while? The one you're seeing now?"

"Well, I'm not actually seeing her . . ."

"You know what I mean. I just want to know if you know who I'm talking about without mentioning her name."

"Yeah, OK, I know who you're talking about."

"Well, I think you also had a pretty good idea that I was seeing someone else at the same time, right?"

"Yeah, I think so."

"You know who I'm talking about?"

"Yes."

"And you remember what happened to her?"

"Yes."

"What I'm wondering is, do you think that will be discovered?"

"Well, it was already discovered," Larry said. "I mean, what happened to her and everything."

"I'm asking you because of the line of work you're in if you think my, um, involvement with her might be discovered. Do you think if someone saw me with her or saw me at her apartment or something, is it possible I would be questioned or anything?"

"It's possible. But you know, that's not the kind of, uh, project my company is into, you know. That's handled by the police."

"I know. I just thought, as a friend, you might be able

to shed some light on that. You know, it would be not too good for me, I mean my career and everything, my reputation, for it to be in the paper that I was even involved with her, let alone if I was under suspicion or something."

"I know what you mean," Larry said.

"What would you think about my turning myself in and just telling someone straight out that I was seeing this girl but that I had nothing to do with what happened to her? Do you think if I did that they could do whatever checking they need to do without it getting in the paper?"

"I don't know. It sounds like a pretty good idea, and you can be sure that if they discover this involvement before you tell *them*, it could be real noisy and make you look worse."

"Listen, Larry, I gotta get back to work here, but I could use some advice on who to talk to and how to go about it, but I don't want to do it by phone. Could I maybe come and see you today?"

Festschrift nodded to Larry.

"Uh, sure. I'll be home all day. You know where I am, don't you?"

"I'll find it. I gotta go. I have to stop by my place first, but I'll try to see you before three."

Larry hung up, folded his arms, leaned back against the kitchen wall, and focused a puzzled stare at Wally.

But Festschrift was already on the radio to Merrill, recounting the entire conversation, almost verbatim. "Well, I think he went for the bait," Merrill said. "But I'll bet he never used that line before to gain entry for one of these jobs."

"Tell him I was almost convinced he was sincere," Larry said.

Wally radioed the message to Merrill.

The answer came back: "Tell superbait not to bet his life on it."

It wasn't funny.

Time: 1:07 P.M.

Merrill: Wally, you there? Over.

Festschrift: Yeah, boss.

Merrill: Shannon called HQ about two minutes ago. Childers has left the office. Let's not buy his story about going home first. You might want to get into position. We're where we can see him if he enters either side of the building. We'll follow him up there, but we'll have to be at least a minute behind him to be safe. By the time he's been in there a minute, we'll likely be right outside the door. But after I tell you he's on his way up, you gotta kill the radio so he doesn't hear any static.

Festschrift: Gotcha. Thanks. Over.

Time: 2:35 P.M.

Merrill: Wally, we're comin' up.

Festschrift: What? What have you got?

Merrill: The jig's up, Wally. It's over.

Festschrift: What're you talkin' about? What's goin' down?!

Merrill: We've got another murder, Wally. Same M.O.

Festschrift: Who?

Merrill: Chuck Childers is dead, Wally. We're comin' up there.

# THIRTEEN

Wally snapped off his radio and tossed it on the couch in the living room. Larry flopped down in a kitchen chair as if he'd been bowled over. I emerged from the closet, cramped and sweaty.

We were speechless. Wally took off his shoulderstrap holster and placed it carefully next to his radio, then sat down, his mass lifting his feet off the floor as he settled in. I leaned over the kitchen table and rested on my hands.

"What now, Wally?" Larry said finally. But Wally just shook his head sadly.

Larry went into the living room and I straightened up and stretched. The phone rang. "Can you get that, Philip?" Larry said.

I picked up the phone. "It's Earl!" I said, and Wally grabbed the extension.

Earl was panting. "You got your radio off up there?"

"Yeah," Wally said.

"I had to run two blocks to this phone! We just spotted Raven. He should be there any second. We're on our way."

Wally hunched himself up off that couch, grabbed his stuff, and lumbered into the dining room. I hung up the phone and jumped back into the closet, pulling the door shut and trying to control my breathing. Larry headed for the kitchen. "Stay in the living room," Wally whispered. "And don't be too quick to answer the door." Less than a minute later the doorbell rang. Larry waited. It rang again. He approached the door and looked out the peephole. "Who is it?" he called out.

"Congratulations, Mr. Shipman," came Jake Raven's deep, resonant voice from the hall. "You've won WMTR-FM's Lucky Bucks Game!"

"Jake, is that you, you old son-of-a-gun?"

"Yeah," Raven said, laughing. "Let me in, turkey!"

Larry opened the door. Raven was not yet in my line of sight. "Hey, for a minute there I thought I'd really won something!" Larry said, a little too loudly. "I s'pose it'd look a little suspicious if your friends won the money though, huh?"

"Yeah, I suppose. Listen, you got a minute?"

Raven's voice sounded farther away, as if he was inviting himself to the living room.

"Yeah, I got some time. C'mon out here and I'll take your coat and find you a beer."

As they entered the kitchen, Larry pointed to the chair in front of my closet and Raven sat down and put a leather briefcase down on the floor beside him. Larry draped Raven's coat on another chair. "What brings you around here, Jake?" he said, opening the refrigerator but careful not to turn his back on his guest.

"Well, believe it or not, I really am giving away one of our prizes today."

"Yeah? In this building?"

"No, down the street, but I remembered you live around here, so I thought I'd stop in and see if you were home. Didn't really expect to see you. You're not workin' today?"

"Nope. Day off," Larry said, popping the top and setting the can before Raven. "I didn't know you got to give the money away."

"Yeah. It's fun. Sometimes it's a thousand or two, you know."

"Yeah, I know."

"Anyway, DJs don't wanna do that kind of work. But I enjoy it. People are thrilled."

Larry slowly sat down across from Raven, stared into his eyes, and said nothing. Raven took a long swallow and set the can down again. Rising, he moved to his left and put his briefcase flat on the counter. Larry started to stand.

"Don't get up," Raven said evenly, his friendly tone gone. "I want to talk to you for a minute."

Larry sat back down, his face taut, one finger tapping silently on the table.

"May I use a towel?" Raven asked. Larry nodded and Raven carefully removed a dish towel from a rod on the wall. Folding it neatly in half, he held it under a stream of water until it was drenched. He pressed the excess water out of it in the sink and set the towel down next to his brief-case. By now I knew he was in Wally's line of vision and that Wally had to have moved a few feet to his right to remain undetected. My breathing was short and shallow.

I strained to get a better view when Raven tripped the spring latches on the briefcase and delicately set the top open. I held my breath, knowing that if he pulled a pistol out of that case, I would have to make my move.

He pulled out two tiny, white gloves, the type film editors use when they're splicing film. Larry watched unblinking as Raven almost daintily tugged the gloves on, and it was then that I noticed the perfection of his clothes.

He wore light brown patent leather shoes, expensive tan slacks that stopped at the top of the heel just so, and a rust colored knit shirt. He looked as if he had just had a shave, and his razor-cut hair was in perfect order. "Is that how you get in, Jake?" Larry asked. "You tell people they've won the radio money prize in that great voice of yours?"

Raven stiffened. "Silence," he said.

"Forget it," Larry said. "You can stand there and blow me away like you have all the others, but you're not gonna tell me I can't ask a few questions."

Raven ignored him and leaned over the table to grab the beer can. He poured the remainder down the sink, ran the water again, wiped his fingerprints off the can and the faucet with his gloved hands, and tossed the can in the trash. Then he wiped his chair and the table and the counter. I wondered how much more we'd need before taking him. Earl and Lieutenant Merrill had to be pressed up against the door by now.

My .38 snub-nose was heavy in my hand, and I wondered if I'd be able to move if I had to. I was ready, but my job was to stay put unless I saw that gun in his hand. And so far, I hadn't even seen the gun.

"Talk to me," Larry said. "Sit down and talk to me."

Raven snorted. "Oh sure," he said. "I have nothing to say to you."

"C'mon, give me a break for old time's sake."

"You think I'm going to come this far and then give you a break?"

"Hey, I'm curious, Jake. At least tell me what the initials mean."

Raven looked genuinely puzzled, as if he really didn't understand what Larry was asking.

"Ohhhh," he said, finally. "You mean these." He reached into his case and produced a bullet with the high velocity slug. "This one's just for you. I had to make two of these today."

My eyes darted to Larry's face, and I saw him press his lips together as if to keep himself from saying, "I know." If he had, even the deranged mind of a Jake Raven would have computed that Larry had inside knowledge and was setting him up.

He played with the bullet in his fingers as he stood towering over Larry, just far enough away that he could thwart a move if Shipman tried anything. "Yes, Larry. The prize trick has worked every time, except I didn't need it for Frances or Chuck."

"Chuck?"

"Chuck."

"Or me."

"Or you."

Raven suddenly clasped the bullet in his fist as if he were through chatting.

Larry spoke. "You've told me this much; at least tell me about the initials."

"If you'd been in L.A. in the sixties you would know."

"I wasn't. I'm sorry."

"I'm sorry too. You missed a great show. I was the morning man. And I was big."

"I'll bet you were."

"Don't patronize me. I *was* big. And my trademark was a cute little closing at the end of my gig every day. At ten o'clock, Pacific Time, I would say, 'Thank you, everyone. Thank you for turning me on.'"

Larry wanted to stall him some more, looking as if he too wondered what Wally was waiting for. Unless I saw the gun, I wasn't going to do anything. Wally was to handle every other eventuality.

"Are you gonna make me beg you to tell me what the initials mean?" Larry said.

Raven laughed a sad laugh and leaned his hips against the counter. "Don't you remember those crazy names we DJs had back then?"

Larry sat silent.

"Well, don't you?"

"Yeah, sure."

"I had a beautiful name. I went by Stacks DeVincent. Stacks DeVincent. Don't you love it?"

And with that, Raven turned his back to me so that he could still watch Larry out of the corner of his eye. He brought the bullet up to the thumb and forefinger of his right hand and reached into his briefcase, which was now blocked from my view, with his left.

Two bounding steps from the dining room entrance shook the whole kitchen and with a loud grunting shout Wally Festschrift smothered Raven with a crashing bear hug, driving him across the kitchen into the far corner where I heard flesh and bone give way against the lip of the formica counter top.

Upon the initial impact I blasted out of the closet as Larry went under the table, and Merrill and Earl came through the front door in low crouches, guns up. With my gun barrel pressed against Raven's forehead on the floor, I searched frantically for his weapon. It had clanged into the sink, the lone bullet spinning into the drain basket. He never got the bullet into the chamber.

Still astride the writhing Raven, whose face mirrored the pain of that blow against the counter, Wally fished handcuffs out of his belt. When Earl saw Raven's right forearm, however, he told Wally, "Just cuff his left to your right. He's goin' nowhere."

Raven's right wrist and hand jutted out at a cockeyed

angle and his forearm appeared crushed. As Wally helped him up, ignoring the yelps of pain, he thrust his hand into the crying man's rib cage. "He's got some severe damage here, too," he said.

Before Earl and Larry and I left the precinct house downtown that night, Wally came out to say good-bye. I was still shaken. So was Larry. I'm sure he was as eager to see Shannon as I was to see Margo.

Wally shook hands with Larry first. Neither spoke. Then Wally grabbed my hand and smacked me on the shoulder with his free hand, almost knocking me off balance. "Be glad you're not in the kitchen," he said with a big smile.

As he took Earl's hand and threw his arm around his neck, Haymeyer said, "Wally, you're something, you know that?"

"Yeah, I know that," the big man said. "You're really gonna think I'm somethin' when you find out what I got us roped into." He winked at me.

"What's this?" Earl said, trying to break free of Wally's grasp. Wally wasn't budging.

"I made a deal with the kid over here," he said, "but you're part of the bargain."

"You can't make a deal for me," Earl said, still buried in Wally's embrace.

"Well, maybe I can't, but I did, and a Festschrift deal is a deal. Right, Philip?"

I nodded.

"Tell your sweetie that your boss and me will see you Sunday, huh?"

I nodded again.

# ABOUT THE AUTHOR

Jerry Jenkins is a widely published author of biographies and children's fiction. He has written the biographies of Orel Hershiser (on the New York Times Bestseller list for nine weeks), Meadowlark Lemon, Hank Aaron, Walter Payton, B. J. Thomas, Dick Motta, Luis Palau, and Deanna McClary.

Many of Jenkins' eighty books have topped the religious bestseller lists. His articles have been published in *Reader's Digest, The Saturday Evening Post,* and virtually every major Christian magazine.

Jenkins is currently the editor of *Moody Monthly* and writer-in-residence at Moody Bible Institute. Born in Kalamazoo, Michigan, he lives on a farm in Zion, Illinois, with his wife, Dianna, and their three sons, Dallas, Chad, and Michael.